For Jack Williams

I would also like to acknowledge the great help I have had from Joanna Kelly, former Governor of Holloway Prison, and her book, *When the Gate Shuts*.

FELICITY DOUGLAS

Also by Felicity Douglas

WITHIN THESE WALLS, BOOK 1

Felicity Douglas

Within These Walls: The Governor

Futura Publications Limited

A Futura Book

First published in Great Britain in 1975
simultaneously by Arthur Barker Limited
and Futura Publications Limited

This book is based on the scripts by David Butler
and Felicity Douglas for the London Weekend Television
series 'Within These Walls'

ISBN 0 8600 7248 7

Printed in Great Britain by
Hazell Watson & Viney Ltd
Aylesbury, Bucks

Futura Publications Limited
Warner Road, London SE5

CHAPTER ONE

A cold grey November morning, with the street lights still on. Stone Park prison loomed up out of the early morning mist, forbidding, unwelcoming.

The Governor, Faye Boswell, was just leaving her house when the telephone rang, that urgent compelling bell which is so hard to ignore. For a moment she was tempted to disregard it. Then she turned and went back. Bill might be ringing her from Beirut.

It was not her husband however, but Cecily Foyle. Cecily had been at college with Faye and now, at Faye's suggestion, had become a prison visitor. She was ringing to ask if she could look in and see Faye after work that evening. She wanted her advice.

'Of course,' said Faye. 'About seven? You could stay and have a bite to eat.'

'Fine. Is Bill still away?' asked Cecily.

'Yes. Nearly four weeks,' said Faye, and heard the depression in her voice. It was stupid to miss her husband so much after so many years of marriage.

The fact was, she thought, that when Bill was away she became too deeply absorbed in the prison and all its problems.

The prison was beginning to come to life. The day staff had been on duty for over an hour. On the Wings, the women were having breakfast. In the South Wing, the atmosphere was fairly calm, almost subdued. Martha Parrish, the Assistant Governor of this Wing was a noted disciplinarian and was proud that hers was known as 'The Quiet Wing'.

In the Remand Wing, the atmosphere was more tense.

Here were lodged the women who were on remand, awaiting trial: some were only here for a few days or a week: some, if their cases were complicated, might be here for some months. In one of the cells a new inmate sobbed bitterly. In many ways it was the saddest place in the whole prison.

The most cheerful place – if anywhere in a prison can be called cheerful – was the Maternity Wing, known officially as K block. It was not part of the prison proper, but was a house, once the prison officers' quarters, which had been converted into a hostel for the prisoners who had their babies with them. This morning the mothers had had their breakfasts and were washing and dressing their babies. In the nursery the atmosphere was nearer to normal than anywhere else in the prison. The mothers, most of whom were very young, laughed and talked and argued as they looked after their babies. Only one of them seemed deeply unhappy. As she dressed her three months old baby, tears rolled slowly down her cheeks. Sister, who missed very little, went across to her.

'You can still change your mind, Sandra,' she said to the disturbed young mother. 'You can keep him here if you prefer.'

Sandra shook her head.

'No,' she said, 'he cried again all last night. It's better for him to go. He hates it here so much.'

Two of the other mothers, both sharp looking girls, exchanged glances.

'She's wet,' one of them muttered and the other replied, 'As if a kid of three months could know he was in the Nick.'

And both girls collapsed into a fit of giggles.

'That's enough,' said Sister sharply; and the giggling stopped. Sister took Sandra's baby into the next room to put him into his pram, until the foster mother came to fetch him. She did not herself think it was advisable to send the baby away, but both Peter Mayes, the senior medical officer, and the head psychiatrist had recommended it, and it was not for her to say otherwise.

On the North Wing there was as usual a great deal of noise and laughter and argument added to the clatter of knives and forks on the tin plates which the authorities so thoughtfully provided. This Wing had a far younger Assistant Governor, Janet Harker, who believed in giving her charges as much freedom as possible, with the result that, although squabbles were frequent and fights were not unknown, the inmates were on the whole less tense than those on the other Wings.

Mrs Armitage, the Chief Officer, did not approve of Miss Harker's methods, for she belonged to the old school; and while the inmates responded to her tough discipline, it was Janet Harker who was the most popular Assistant Governor in the whole prison.

This morning Pat Berryman, a newly recruited prison officer, was talking to Janet in her office at the end of the Wing.

'Don't look now,' she said, 'but old Lizzie is letting Vi have most of her breakfast.'

Vi was an enormously fat woman with an insatiable appetite. She invariably sat as near to old Lizzie Brough as possible, knowing there would be some pickings.

Janet Harker wandered out into the Wing, to be greeted cheerfully by some of the women and rudely by others. When she got to Lizzie's place she paused.

'Feeling all right, Lizzie?' she asked.

'Me indigestion's bad today, miss,' said Lizzie cheerfully.

Like all the much older prisoners, she did not really mind being inside and had made her cell a home from home.

'I don't fancy anythink much. Still my loss is Vi's gain,' she added as the gross woman tucked into a second breakfast.

Miss Harker smiled, and then said seriously. 'You ought

to see the doctor again. I'll put you on the list of medical applications.'

'Don't you do that Miss,' said Lizzie. 'I don't want to be forever bothering him.' And then to her fat friend, 'Hey! Don't drink all my tea, I want that for myself.'

Janet decided not to make an issue of it and called a prison officer to bring Lizzie another cup: and after scolding Vi (a scolding which would not have the slightest effect as she well knew), she went back into her office.

Outside it was now light. Another day at Stone Park had begun.

Charles Radley, the Deputy Governor, was going to be late for work. As he was a rigidly punctual man this was unusual. It was unusual that he should be thinking about anything at this time of day except his work. He was something of a career man, hoping that in time he would have his own prison. During the past two years he had concentrated almost entirely on Stone Park, taking his work home at night and leaving early each morning. This was partly because of his ambition and partly because of his unhappy marriage.

His wife Beth had bitterly resented the demands his work made on him. The Governor, who liked both of the Radleys, had realised that something had gone very wrong and last summer had more or less bullied him into taking Beth on a holiday in the hills of Provence, instead of going, as usual, to one or other of their somewhat boring parents. The result was totally unexpected; Charles had fallen in love with Beth all over again. Indeed he realized now that he had not been in love with her when they first married.

On their return from holiday Beth had given up her work as teacher at an infants school and instead had taken a part time job in a play group. But this morning she had told Charles that she was expecting a baby: he had not known whether to be glad or sorry. The past year had been the happiest he had known; they had been out together more than ever before in all their years of marriage; and they had had friends in in the evenings. Charles realized that in some way his work as Deputy had benefited from the fact that he no longer thought of absolutely nothing except Stone Park, with its three hundred odd inmates and its consequent problems.

He waited to leave in order to drop Beth at her play group and kissed her goodbye.

'Take care,' he said. 'And rest when you get in.'

'Fusspot,' said Beth and smiled at him.

As she got out he said, 'Hey! Shall I tell Faye and Peter Mayes?'

'Not yet. Wait till I begin to bulge.' And she added 'Goodbye – Daddy.'

As he drove away, Charles Radley felt a masculine elation in the fact that he was to become a father. If Beth agreed, they would ask Faye to be godmother. After all, if it hadn't been for her, this might never have happened.

As Faye drove towards the prison, her thoughts wandered back over the two years since she had first been appointed Governor. Despite her liberal ideas and reforming zeal, she had begun to feel that she had not after all achieved much in those years.

True, she had introduced, with difficulty, certain improvements in the inmates' lot, but prison was prison; and until there was space and money enough to separate the very young from the habitual criminals, and to segregate the feeble minded and the drunks, it was bound to be an unhappy and depressing place.

The authorities themselves were basing the concept of the new prison, to be built during the next ten years, on the theory that 'Conventional prisons are unnecessary for the vast majority of women, whose offences are mainly due to personality disorders.' Miss Clarke, the Welfare Officer, had been delighted when she heard of this, for it was in line with her whole way of thinking. On the other hand, Mrs Armitage, the Chief Officer, had snorted, saying, in her downright way, 'If you ask me, Madam, most of the women would sooner be thought bad than mad.'

Faye had smiled to herself. Although there was a constant though unacknowledged conflict between herself and the Chief, Faye had grown fond of her, and could not deny that she was a tower of strength, who understood the inmates as well, if not better, than the highly trained welfare officers.

When Faye arrived in her office she found a larger post than usual waiting for her. She also found that Penny, her secretary, had some coffee ready for her. She drank it gratefully. When Bill was away she was apt to leave for work on an empty stomach. 'Bless you, Penny,' she said.

In a business like way she told Penny whom to summon to the staff meeting that morning. She had half an hour before taking Disciplinary and Applications.

'Pull yourself together, and stop feeling depressed. Bill will ring,' she admonished herself firmly; and applied herself to her work.

CHAPTER TWO

In the Maternity Ward, Sandra Logan was nursing her baby. Sandra was a pale rather beautiful eighteen year old. Her baby was plain and unattractive; but Sandra firmly believed that no more lovely child had ever been born. And now she was going to lose him.

Sister Lin came into the room.

'The car is here to take him, Sandra,' she said.

Sandra held him more closely than ever. Sister looked at her gravely. 'You can still change your mind,' she said gently.

There was a pause. Then Sandra shook her head.

'They'll look after him proper?'

'Of course. We know them well. We have sent them babies before. And if he's going, he must go now . . . we mustn't keep the car waiting.'

With a pitiful gesture Sandra pressed the baby into Sister's arms, and then turned and ran from the room. With a puzzled look, Sister took the baby out to the waiting car, while upstairs in her bedroom Sandra sat in dumb misery.

When Sister went up half an hour later she found her still in great distress.

'I shall have to take her to see Dr Mayes,' Sister thought and went to the telephone to ring the surgery.

The Assistant Governor of North Wing, Janet Harker, was sitting in her small office checking through the lists of transfers and discharges. The Chief Officer was with her.

'That's two to be transferred to Merton on Friday, and

Maggie Williams to be taken to her home visit. But I believe Mrs Boswell has arranged that,' said Janet.

Mrs Armitage nodded. 'Yes. Mrs Foyle is taking her. Maggie is due for discharge in three weeks. Which day is it exactly?'

Janet consulted a list. 'The twenty-fourth – full remission.'

'I'll double check with the office.'

Janet smiled. 'Don't you trust my calculations?'

'I like to make sure. If anyone is kept in even one day longer than she should be, all hell breaks loose.'

'I bet it does. Have you ever known it happen?'

Mrs Armitage smiled grimly. 'Only once. Two women with the same surname and initials got mixed up. It cost the department a pretty penny in compensation.'

Janet laughed. 'No wonder you are careful to check.'

A Redband, Vivien Pearce, was in the doorway.

'What is it, Vivien?' asked Janet.

'I've come for the medical reports for Dr Mayes. You told me to take them down.'

'Of course. Here they are.' She handed a folder to Vivien. 'You've got your home visit soon haven't you?'

'In three weeks.'

'Looking forward to it?'

'That's putting it mildly. It'll be grand to see my mother at home instead of in the visiting room. She's been wonderful to me over all this wretched business.'

Mrs Armitage listened rather grimly. She herself was not in the habit of chatting the prisoners up. Miss Harker gave Vivien a smile and the file and Vivien left.

'She's a nice girl, quiet, toes the line, reliable. If only more of them were like that,' said Janet.

'M-m' said Mrs Armitage.

'You sound doubtful.'

'Do I? I just wonder what's really going on inside her.'

'In fact you don't trust her.' Janet smiled, rather sadly.

'I don't trust anyone. Nor will you when you've been in the Prison Service as long as I have.'

Janet was about to protest when there was a knock on the door and Pat Berryman, the new prison officer, looked in. She was a cheerful woman who managed to get on with the inmates without being too severe. Even Mrs Armitage admitted that Berryman had the makings of a good officer, though she did not altogether trust her and also had good reason to believe that she sometimes indulged in an odd cigarette while on duty, which was strictly forbidden.

'Excuse me butting in, Miss Harker, but the Governor and the Dep are on their round; they'll be here soon.'

'Thank you Pat,' said Janet Harker. 'All well at your end of the Wing?'

'Yes. Except that old Lizzie is moaning about her indigestion again. I think she ought to apply to see Dr Mayes.'

'She's seen him already,' said Mrs Armitage briefly. 'Lizzie's always been a moaner.'

Pat Berryman looked annoyed, but Janet answered, 'Put her on the list for tomorrow, Pat. I'll have a word with her later on today.'

'Thanks,' said Pat Berryman gratefully and left.

There was a moment's silence between the two women. 'The Chief is in a really bad mood this morning,' Janet thought. Had she known it, Mrs Armitage had had a very disturbed night, with her husband suffering one of his recurrent bouts of pain, and as a result had hardly any sleep at all.

There was a knock on the open door. The Governor and the Deputy came in. Janet noticed that Charles Radley appeared somewhat distrait. 'What's the matter with everyone this morning?' she thought, but aloud she only said, 'Good morning Madam.'

'Good morning Janet, Chief,' said Faye.

Charles Radley nodded.

'Any problems?' asked Faye.

'I don't think so – for once,' answered Janet.

'Good . . . I wanted to ask you about Lily Hever.'

'Have you seen her application? It only went in this morning,' said Janet.

'What was it for?' asked Charles Radley, though he guessed the answer.

'Rule 43 again. Another month in solitary.'

Rule 43 is the rule whereby a prisoner can ask to be locked in her cell, by her own wish. Lily Hever had first asked for it as protection from another prisoner who had every reason to hate her and was inside for GBH.

'Surely she'll have served her time soon?' asked Faye.

'In about six months,' said the Chief.

'She wants to walk straight out of her cell and through the front gates,' said Janet.

'She's afraid of the other women, Madam,' added Mrs Armitage.

'I'm not surprised,' thought Faye, but aloud she said: 'I'm not even going to consider that application until we've discussed it thoroughly. I'll see you both later.'

She turned and walked away, talking to her Deputy. Mrs Armitage looked after her. 'She doesn't realise it,' thought the Chief, 'but she's a great deal tougher than she used to be. As she passed Lily Hever's cell, Faye paused for a moment. She was troubled at the thought of the embittered woman locked into her cell. She moved on and spoke quietly.

'How often has she applied for Rule 43, Charles?'

'Four times in the last year,' said Radley. 'She gets hysterical at the thought of coming out. One can't reason with her.'

'Perhaps we haven't tried hard enough,' answered Faye.

Later on their rounds, as they passed the hospital corridor, Sandra came out of Dr Mayes' surgery, with a nurse supporting her. She did not look up but walked, despondent, with her head bent. Her face was swollen and distorted from crying. After a moment the doctor himself came out of surgery wearing his white coat.

'Morning Peter,' said Radley. 'Wasn't that Sandra Logan?'

'Yes. She's pretty distressed. Her baby was taken to its foster home this morning.'

'Poor girl,' said Faye sympathetically.

'It was entirely her own decision,' said Radley dryly.

'I don't imagine she realised what it would feel like when he was sent away.'

'She's a basically stupid girl,' Radley said.

'Not an easy case,' said Peter Mayes. He sounded puzzled. 'The problem now is whether the distress caused by the loss of the child will be worse than the strain of having him here. She was obsessed by the idea that the infant knew he was in prison, which is absurd.'

'I'll have to be advised by you, Peter,' said Faye, 'We'll talk later at the staff meeting and see what Sister Lin has to say.'

Vivien Pearce was coming towards them. The Governor was genuinely pleased to see her. If all the prisoners were like this girl, what a pleasant task hers would be. 'Hallo Vivien,' she said.

'Good morning madam.' Viven had a wide and infectious smile.

'Not sickening for anything, I hope?' said Radley.

Vivien laughed. 'No sir. I've brought the list of medical applications.' And she handed the file to the doctor.

'Good,' said Faye. 'We wouldn't like you to come down with anything just before you have your weekend at home. Mrs Foyle is going to drive you.'

'Thank you, Madam.'

'I'm sure your visit will go well. But if there are any difficulties don't hesitate to come and see me when you get back.'

'Thank you. But I think everything will go well. I've got super parents.'

As she went away both Faye and Charles Radley looked after her and wished that more of their charges had Vivien's pleasant manner and also her reliability.

At the Staff Conference Peter Mayes raised the question of Sandra Logan, who would now have to be transferred from Maternity to one of the Wings. Faye decided that North Wing would be best for her, but Janet Harker protested that she had no room for the girl, unless she put her in to share with Vivien Pearce, who, as a Redband, enjoyed the privilege of a cell to herself.

'Why not?' said Faye. 'She is such a nice girl and she might be able to help Sandra at this juncture.'

'A bit hard on her,' said Radley.

'I don't think she'll mind,' said Faye. 'She is so co-operative.'

Some demon prompted Peter Mayes to say, 'You could always put her in with Lily Hever.'

There was a distinct reaction from the staff, as though he had said something obscene. Lily Hever was a woman whom nobody liked or trusted. She had by bullying caused the death of a young girl, Norah, who had jumped into the net rather than share with her. Miss Parrish, who had sat with Norah while she died, had never forgiven Lily. Her lips were tighter than usual when she spoke.

'Not a very good joke, Doctor, if I may say so.'

Faye disregarded this and said coolly, 'I had been going to speak of Lily Hever. She has spent so much of the last year in solitary confinement, at her own request.'

'And for her protection from the other women,' added the Chief.

'Of course. But I think it is now time she came out.'

Mrs Armitage's face was flushed. This was a subject on which she felt very strongly.

'If Lily Hever comes out,' she said, 'everyone in this room will regret it. I've had too much experience of that one.'

'I too have had some experience of her,' said Faye. She did not sound pleased.

'I think what Mrs Armitage means is that nothing will change Lily now,' said Miss Parrish. 'It has all been tried. She is not intelligent, but she is cunning and a trouble maker.'

The Chief was grateful for her colleague's support and added:

'She's also a persistent malingerer. She steals from the other women and intimidates the weaker ones.'

'Surely you haven't forgotten poor little Norah, madam?' asked Miss Parrish.

'I haven't forgotten,' said Faye.

'Not to mention the time she shopped Margie Bassett,' said Radley.

'I know,' said Faye, 'that's all true. But what do we do? Write her off as an incurable statistic? Do we only help when we're certain of success?'

'You can't help Lily Hever. She's beyond it. The country's better off with her in prison; and the prison's a healthier place with her locked up on her own.' Mrs Armitage spoke with conviction.

There was a pause. Faye realised that few of her staff agreed with her over Lily Hever.

'I am aware that we have failed with Lily,' she said, 'but I still want to do what's best for her.'

'We can't even guarantee her safety, if we force her to come out,' Mrs Armitage was speaking very emphatically indeed. 'Once she's out she'll make trouble some way. In my opinion it's not worth the risk.'

'What do you think, Mr Radley?' Faye asked.

Privately he thought Faye was making a deal too much fuss over the whole thing, but naturally did not say so.

'Obviously it's bad for her to be completely segregated,' he answered. 'But I don't know what the alternative is. My own feeling is to leave her where she is.

'I'm sorry,' said Faye firmly. 'I know I'm in a minority over this. But it is time that Lily came out. I will speak to her myself later today.'

When Janet Harket got back to the Wing she had a word with Vivien about sharing with Sandra. As a Redband, the girl had had a room to herself but, as Janet had anticipated, she proved very co-operative. Janet put her in the picture regarding Sandra, and thought she would probably be able to help the girl.

She sent an officer to fetch Sandra, who had been resting since the Doctor had given her a sedative. She now seemed calmer, although she was still very withdrawn and quiet. Janet took her along to Vivien's cell and told her to wait outside.

Another bed had been moved in. Vivien was sitting at her table writing a letter. As Janet entered she stood up.

'It's all right, Vivien. I've brought Sandra along. She's a bit upset and should be left alone for a few days to adjust. Do what you can for her.'

'Of course I will.'

'I'm so grateful to you.' Miss Harker went to the door and called Sandra.

'Should I mention the baby to her?' asked Vivien quietly.

'Play it by ear.'

Sandra came in, carrying her holdall. She seemed shut in on herself, detached, as if nothing that was happening to her had any real meaning.

'Sandra Logan – Vivien Pearce. I'll leave you together.'

And Janet Harker went out.

There was a pause. Sandra stood, clutching her holdall. She seemed almost afraid to look at Vivien.

'Sit down,' said the older girl. 'That's your bed. Like a cup of tea?' Sandra shook her head. 'Then I'll leave you alone for a bit. I'll be just outside if you want anything. I'll bring you some food when it comes up.'

She went out. She noticed that Sandra was hugging her holdall as though it was her baby. 'Poor kid,' she thought. 'Why ever did she let the baby go?'

When the staff meeting was over Faye moved from her desk and went to stand at the window. Outside it was still a grey unhappy day. She thought with some envy of Bill who was probably working in the sun. He had neither written nor rung her for over a week and she had begun to fight a feeling of anxiety, though she knew that, had he been ill, she would have been told at once. She heard the telephone in the next room, and, faintly, Penny's voice answering it. Then, a knock on the door and Penny herself came in.

'It's an overseas call for you Mrs Boswell,' she said. 'Person to person. They are holding on.'

'Thank you Penny,' said Faye, and went to the telephone.

'Mrs Boswell speaking,' she said, telling herself not to panic. After a moment of clicks and buzzings she heard, to her great relief, Bill's voice.

'That you darling?'

'Bill!' said Faye thankfully.

'I rang you last evening but you weren't in,' said the familiar voice. 'I left Beirut yesterday. I'm in Basle now. I've got a meeting at lunch time but I should be through in time to catch the afternoon plane. I'll be home eightish or so. All right?'

'All right indeed,' said Faye. 'Shall I meet you?'

'No. I'll make my own way. Bless you. See you soon.'

Faye rang off, smiling, feeling, as she had to admit to herself, quite idiotically pleased at the knowledge that Bill was coming home again.

'Now for Lily Hever,' she said and went briskly towards North Wing.

Lily Hever was standing in her cell, her ear pressed against the key hole, listening to the footsteps and voices from outside. Although she was locked in at her own wish, she was very lonely and sometimes longed for companionship. Not for friendship, for that was outside Lily's ken. Rather to be able to make herself felt, to upset and torment her fellow prisoners. But even stronger than this longing was her fear of them.

Once she had been nearly killed by one of them, 'Big Fran,' for shopping a girl she had befriended. It was then that Lily had originally asked for Rule 43. She had been out of her cell several times since then, but each time she had in one way or another aroused the hostility of the other women and had fled again to her sanctuary.

She heard the grating of the key in the lock of her cell. She bolted back and sat on the bed, her hands demurely folded on her lap. The door opened. The Governor and Mrs Armitage stood there. The Governor came in. The Chief moved away, only just out of sight and well within hearing. She did not trust Lily Hever further than she could see her, and disapproved deeply of her Governor's attitude over this particular prisoner.

As Faye came in, Lily rose apprehensively.

'Good morning madam,' she said, cringing a little, as was her way with the Governor. A wave of dislike came over Faye. She had a sudden impulse to forgo her errand, to bow to her colleagues' opinions and to forget her intention to bring Lily back into the life of the prison. She could so easily pretend that she had only come to pass the time of day, to pay Lily her statutory visit, and then pass on. What was it that Mrs Armitage had said? 'The prison's a healthier place with her locked up.' For a moment Faye was really tempted, and then her native obstinacy reasserted itself. Disagreeable as this woman was, Faye was still responsible for her well-being, and she was convinced that to send anyone straight out into the world after months of solitary confinement would be an unwise, even cruel thing to do.

She hoped her dislike of Lily did not show too much. She forced a small smile and said, 'Good morning Lily.'

'Take my chair, madam,' said Lily in her obsequious way, with one of those sidelong glances which Faye disliked so much.

The two women sat facing each other; the elder one controlled and handsome, well groomed and well dressed; the younger slovenly, untidy, almost uncouth in her shabby uniform cardigan and skirt, the prison pallor very evident. Only her dark eyes showed that nature had intended her, too, to be a handsome woman.

Lily spoke again. 'It's ever so good of you to visit me, madam. But then you always have been considerate.'

She was speaking with care, using what she thought of as her posh voice, which she could turn on at will. She was also smiling in her usual ingratiating way. Faye did not smile back.

'I expect you know why I've come to see you.'

'About my application?'

'Yes.'

'It's the last time, madam. I'm due for release in six months and if I can stay here in peace till then I'd be ever so grateful.'

'I'm sorry Lily, but I'm not going to agree to your application.'

This was entirely unexpected, and Lily's careful accent

slipped. 'I'm not going back into bloody association! I want to be on me own.'

She had risen and was shouting at Faye. Outside Mrs Armitage moved nearer the door.

'I'm afraid it's not possible,' answered Faye quietly.

'I want Rule 43! It's my right!'

And in this she was speaking only the truth.

'Sit down Lily.' Faye's voice was stern. 'When your sentence is over you will be going out into the world.'

'Roll on, you old cow,' muttered Lily rudely. Faye deliberately ignored this.

'You've served quite a long sentence. Have you considered what it will be like, being exposed to people and traffic; going into shops and cafés, doing a job? All these things are worrying enough when you've been inside. If you went to them straight from solitary it might be too much for you to bear. Have you thought of that?'

'I know what to expect,' answered Lily sulkily.

'Perhaps. But it would be much less shock if you had been outside this cell, with the others on the Wing.'

There was a pause. Even Lily could see the truth in what the Governor was telling her, and realised that she was trying to help her. Then she heard a raucous laugh from outside and cringed again.

'It's them out there madam. You don't know what they're like. There's two or three of them just waiting to mark me.

'Nonsense,' said Faye firmly. 'Fran is the only one left who was here with you; and she's very near the end of her sentence. She won't want to lose her remission on your account; she'll leave you alone.'

'What about that woman Kyle?' asked Lily nervously.

Faye was not surprised that Lily sounded nervous. Kyle was a political prisoner on whom Lily had played a particularly dirty trick by first befriending and helping her and later, for her own purposes, giving her away to the authorities. Fortunately Kyle was now on the Long Term Wing and would never meet Lily, as Faye now told her, adding, 'When you come out, the officers will be watching. At any sign of trouble they'll move in.'

'Protection, eh?' said Lily. The idea boosted her ego.

'They'll see you are safe,' said Faye, wondering why she was so patient with Lily.

'Well . . . if you'll guarantee it madam.'

'All I can guarantee is that you'll come to no harm if you behave.'

Lily gave one of her insincere smiles.

'What would I make trouble for?'

Faye had suddenly had enough. She rose. 'Right. I'll let Miss Harker know that you are to come out tomorrow,' and without further ado she left the cell.

CHAPTER THREE

Vivien watched the Governor and Mrs Armitage walk away together, after locking the door on Lily again. She noticed that the Chief's face was flushed with anger and that Mrs Boswell seemed preoccupied. She wondered if there was any truth in the rumour that Lily would be coming out? For Lily's sake she hoped it was true, and not one of the many rumours which circulated the prison, for surely it was not good for anyone to be alone for such long periods? But for the sake of everyone else she hoped that Lily would remain inside.

Vivien had been on the Wing with her for a short while at the beginning of her sentence, and she had discovered that the woman was an inveterate trouble maker, besides being a habitual thief. She was also utterly lacking in any sort of sympathy with her companions in their troubles. The long term prisoners told a story of a young girl, Norah, whom Lily had terrorised to such an extent that she had been driven to suicide. There were other stories too. Vivien could not help being sorry for the wretched woman but she prayed that the authorities would not let her out.

It was a quiet time of day on the Wing. The working parties had not returned. One or two elderly inmates pottered round, and in her cell Sandra seemed to be dozing. Poor girl, thought Vivien, she certainly seems worn out. However much she misses the baby, at least she will get some sleep now he has gone away. She'll find it different on the Wing though. In Maternity, which was not part of the prison proper, the rooms were in fact real bedrooms, not cells with painted brick walls, in many cases covered with scribbled obscenities by their owners. The noise of the Wing could be frightening at times too.

Vivien's mind returned to her first days on the Wing. She had later been told by some of the officers that she had impressed them by the way in which she had settled down so quickly, without any of the usual traumas which the average prisoner suffers.

If they had only known. She had been in such a state of inner turmoil that she was thankful to be shut away in here. She did not think that she could have borne it, if she had been in the outside world after the shock she had sustained.

To have been forced to make decisions at work, to have seen her friends, (or to have found excuses not to see them) would have been quite beyond her. In prison, despite its many disadvantages, its institutional food, its lack of privacy, she was able to live in a kind of limbo; doing exactly as she was told, completely cut off from the world. And in this way she had regained her sanity.

Her story was in essence an ordinary enough one. One which Faye Boswell, as Prison Governor, heard every day of her life. She had fallen in love with the wrong man, a man who was not of her world, and who had come near to ruining her life.

Miss Berryman passed and spoke to her. For a moment she did not answer, she was far away, then with a jerk she came back to reality, and answered.

The women, who had gone from work to exercise, were beginning to drift back now and the Wing was becoming noisy. The midday meal came up, and Vivien took some in to Sandra. They ate it together in the cell. The girl seemed a little less withdrawn and was obviously wanting to talk about her baby. Vivien let her, thinking it would do her good.

When they had finished eating, Sandra produced a number of snapshots and showed them to Vivien, who thought privately that it was a pity the baby was such a pale and uninteresting looking child. But Sandra was saying proudly:

'He's ever so pretty. But he's a real little boy too. I shall miss him terrible.'

'If you are going to miss him so much, why did you have him sent away?'

'I had to. He cried all night. I was afraid he'd get ill. And now he's with strangers.'

The girl looked so distressed that Vivien said in a consoling way:

'Don't worry. If Miss Clarke arranged it, it will be someone who treats him well.'

'But think how he'll miss me. And it's another six months. He may not know me when I get out.'

Vivien thought this was extremely likely, but managed to convince Sandra that the months would pass quickly. Tomorrow, she thought, she would suggest that Sandra did a domestic science course; but for the moment she would let her relax. She suggested that Sandra might like to watch television after the afternoon work session, and, with her usual lack of enthusiasm, Sandra agreed.

Later that afternoon Faye had arranged to meet someone from the Home Office and take him on a tour of the prison. They started by visiting some of the recreational classes. As usual, the dressmaking and toymaking were well attended; and also, Faye was glad to see, the Current Affairs group which she had lately instigated seemed to be arousing quite a lot of interest. She had always felt that it was wrong that women in prison should know so little of the world outside, which put them at an instant disadvantage when they left – a disadvantage which television had also done much to mitigate.

She was fully aware that Mrs Armitage thought her preoccupation with the aftercare of the prisoners was time wasting and almost frivolous. The Chief's attitude was, 'Keep 'em quiet, keep 'em locked up and don't worry about afterwards;

the chances are they'll be back soon enough,' an attitude which Faye found unconstructive and short sighted.

As they walked towards the Centre Faye's companion remarked on the excellence of some of the toys that were being made. 'Positively professional,' he said and added confidentially:

'Off the record, I have always believed that prisoners – male and female – should be paid for their work at the going rates. Part of their earnings could be banked against their release, and part deducted as a contribution towards their keep, which would be a pleasant relief for the long suffering taxpayer.'

Faye felt in complete agreement with him over this, but all she said, with some bitterness, was, 'Tell that to the Unions!'

Peter Mayes was waiting for them in the Centre. He was to take the visitor to see the Drug Unit.

'When you have finished, come to my office for a cup of tea – Earl Grey, not prison brew,' Faye said.

She turned and crossed the Centre, unlocked the gate and entered North Wing, where the women who did not choose to go to classes were in association.

A few of the women greeted her either with genuine pleasure or a bored shrug. But many of them were watching television and did not acknowledge her and some of the newer admissions, who had had their initial interview with the Deputy Governor, did not even know who she was. With over three hundred inmates and a constantly changing population it was quite impossible for her to have close personal contact with more than a small proportion of them. For instance, although she had constantly discussed the case of Sandra Logan with the Welfare Officers and Sister Lin and knew a great deal about the girl, she would not have recognised her if she had seen her. This deficiency she now proposed to remedy.

She made her way to Janet Harker's office. The Assistant Governor was reading a letter, which she hastily folded and put away in the pocket of her jacket. Faye smiled inwardly. Janet had always had her share of admirers, but it was now an open secret among the staff that she was on the verge of getting engaged to a doctor at one of the big teaching hospitals, an attractive and ambitious young man called Richard something-or-other. Faye had forgotten his surname. Janet would make a good consultant's wife. She also made an excellent assistant governor and Faye could only hope that her marriage would not necessarily mean her resignation. However this was not the moment to discuss it.

Faye smiled and asked how Sandra was getting on.

'She's watching television,' said Janet, 'over there in the big armchair. Vivien's sitting on the arm. See?'

Faye looked at the girl. 'She looks half asleep,' she said.

'Not surprising, the baby yelled all night,' said Janet.

As they spoke, Vivien pulled Sandra to her feet and led her to their cell. They saw the elder girl put a cover over the younger one, as she lay on her bed. Sandra was indeed on the verge of sleep.

Faye remarked on how pretty the girl was, despite her pallor and the signs of exhaustion.

'Too pretty really,' said Janet. 'She's no home and no husband; and with the wretched baby to look after one can't see much future for her.'

'I must get Miss Clarke on to her case.'

'Vivien was talking to me about her earlier this afternoon. She wondered if Sandra could do a domestic science course. Then she might get a job where she could keep the baby with her.'

'It sounds a good idea, if Sandra's prepared to co-operate. Really, Vivien is quite remarkable, concerning herself with a fellow prisoner to that extent, when she hardly knows the girl.'

As they spoke, the girl herself came out of the cell and

quietly shut the door. Then, after a word with Officer Berryman, went quickly off on some errand.

'It's a pity about Vivien,' said Janet. 'She'd make a good welfare officer. She's genuinely interested in after care. Not much chance, I suppose?'

'Unlikely,' said Faye, 'but she had a very good position before she came here. I don't mind betting that whatever she takes up she'll do well.'

Faye was about to go, but paused, as Berryman unlocked the gate for another prisoner, a small woman of forty-five, quietly dressed, with black hair neatly parted in the middle. She seemed out of place and thirty years out of date among the rest of the women, with their trousers or long skirts, their make-up and sometimes bizarre hair arrangements.

'Who is that?' Faye asked.

'That's Reba. Reba Jowett. She's a recidivist. You must remember her.'

'I do now. She's in for fraud, isn't she?'

The woman Reba came towards them. She was carrying a bunch of rather wilted flowers. She nodded politely to Faye, then spoke to Janet.

'I've been doing the flowers in the chapel, miss,' she said meekly. 'The Chaplain asked me to.'

'I know, Reba. And you've taken your time, haven't you?'

'I'm sorry, miss. It's so peaceful down there. These flowers aren't quite finished. Mind if I put them in my room? Seems a shame to throw them away.'

'Very well.'

Faye waited till Reba was out of hearing, then – 'Now there is a woman whom I wouldn't trust one inch.' As she said this, she thought how like her Chief she sounded.

'She's a model prisoner,' answered Janet. 'And I believe she is genuinely devout. I know the Chaplain thinks so.'

'I only hope he's right,' said Faye. 'Keep an eye on the girl

Sandra. I'll go and have a quick word with old Lizzie, then I must get back.'

As the Governor walked away, Janet's hand went to her pocket and took out Richard's letter. She had not finished reading it. She glanced round; the inmates were still intent on their television; Pat Berryman and another officer were well in evidence. She went into her office, opened the letter and read it, a faint colour in her cheeks.

Old Lizzie was dozing in her cell. She had made it almost a home from home; it looked very cosy with quilted cushions on the chairs and a patchwork quilt on the bed. The curtains matched the cushions. On the floor was a rag rug, which Lizzie had also made. She had a long sentence, and had plenty of time to beautify her room. On one wall were two large coloured photographs of the Queen and the Duke of Edinburgh; and on another wall a glamorous one of HRH Mrs Mark Phillips and her husband – and of course her horse. For old Lizzie was a dedicated Royalist.

Faye paused in the door.

'Lizzie,' she said; and then more loudly 'Lizzie – Mrs Brough.'

Lizzie opened her eyes, and after a moment focussed and saw who was visiting her. She was pleased but not overwhelmed. When Lizzie had first come to Stone Park forty years ago the Governor had been a man, and in her heart of hearts she did not really approve of having a woman in charge of the prison. She had also been here when Faye first took over, and felt in some way that this gave her some sort of advantage over the Governor, whom she regarded as a 'new girl'.

Like many of the older inhabitants she was quite content with her lot. Now that her sister had died and her nephew had taken his family to Australia, she had no reason to be outside. She lived from day to day, not thinking of what would happen to her when the time came for her to leave. Some instinct told her she might never leave.

Now she smiled at Mrs Boswell and hastily pushed her teeth into place. She started to rise, but Faye put her hand on her shoulder and pushed her down.

'Don't get up, Lizzie,' she said loudly, knowing the old woman was rather deaf. 'I'll take the other chair.'

'Don't you do that, madam. Sit on the bed. It's more comfortable.'

'But your lovely quilt—?'

'That's all right – for you Madam. Wouldn't let any of the others sit on it.'

'Thank you.' Faye ran her hand over the quilt admiring the workmanship. 'It's beautifully done. You are a good needle-woman Lizzie.'

'It's a gift. I've had it all me life. Not that my eyes are so good now.'

It was ironic, thought Faye, that the same deftness that had made Lizzie such an exquisite needlewoman should also have made her an expert lock picker. All her sentences, and they had been many, had been for 'breaking and entering'.

There was a pause. Then Faye mentioned Lizzie's indigestion. Was it worse? Had she seen the doctor?

'Yes I've seen 'im. He says it's nothing much, just me age. He's given me some nice medicine. Don't you worry, madam.'

'I'm sure Miss Harker will keep an eye on you.'

'Young Janet – begging your pardon m'm – she's a nice girl but she's so young. Like most of the screws. You can't go to them for a bit of advice. It'd be like asking advice from your grandchildren. Why, even you, m'm, you don't look as old as the governors used to.'

She wasn't flattering Faye. Indeed there was a distinct note of disapproval in her voice. Faye felt she had better leave before she bitterly offended old Lizzie by laughing.

'I expect you're right, Lizzie. Well, it's been lovely seeing you, and your room is really nice.' She noticed a large coloured snapshot of children on a beach. 'Your grandchildren?'

'No m'm. I never married.' Proudly. 'I'm Miss Brough. That's m' nephew's kids. Nice i'nt it? Australia, he went to. Doing well. Wanted me to go too but I didn't fancy living with all them blacks.'

Faye wondered whether it was worth explaining to Lizzie that whatever she found in Australia it would not be 'blacks'; and then decided it would be a waste of time. She was just going to leave, when Lizzie said:

'Had a letter from old Georgie Weekes the other week.'

'How is she?' asked Faye.

Mrs Weekes was of the same generation as Lizzie and they had been great friends.

'She's going straight,' Lizzie said. 'Off the shoplifting, and off the drink too. Funny, that is. Georgie always liked her tipple. Don't suppose we'll see her back here again now.' Lizzie sounded regretful.

'I hope not,' said Faye briskly. 'Now, Lizzie, promise me you'll tell the officers if your indigestion gets worse.'

'Yes, m'm. I'll do that.'

But as Faye left, the old woman muttered to herself:

'That doctor! He won't do nothing for me pains. He thinks I'm a skiver.'

CHAPTER FOUR

When Faye's visitor from the Home Office had departed, she put through a call to the Deputy Governor. Mrs Armitage had left early. She did not say why, as she was not in the habit of telling her troubles to the world but in fact she had to take her invalid husband to hospital, for after the great pain he had suffered the night before, the doctors wished to check up.

Faye herself wanted to get back in good time in order to see to Bill's dinner. Now that he was almost home she realised how ridiculously pleased she was at the thought of his return.

There was no reply from Charles Radley, and she was about to put out a general call for him, when his secretary answered, and said that he had left.

Faye was amazed. Charles was perfectly entitled to leave if he wanted, but in all the years she had been at Stone Park, he had never failed to contact her before leaving to find out whether anything urgent had come up during the afternoon, and to discuss plans for the next day. To leave without letting her know was so totally out of character that she wondered whether Charles was ill.

Charles was not ill. He was at that moment buying Beth rather too many extravagant flowers and on the way home, booking a table at their favourite Chinese restaurant. If he had known it, the last thing that Beth wanted to do this evening was to go out, as she was feeling very tired and rather sick, but as he so plainly needed to celebrate, she said nothing and pretended to be pleased. How odd human nature was, she thought; never in a hundred years would she have imagined that Charles would be so delighted at the thought of a baby:

he was obviously going to be a doting father. Beth, who was not the doting kind, hoped she would not find it too irritating.

Faye also bought some flowers on the way home. She was inclined to neglect such things when Bill was away.

She picked up the evening paper which lay on the mat, together with the second post. She noticed there was a letter from Paul from Bangladesh. She put it aside, to read at her leisure, for Paul, like many sons, did not write very often; but when he did, it was usually a long and entertaining epistle.

She had taken some food out of the deep freeze, and had finished arranging the flowers when the front door bell rang. For a moment she wondered who it could be, and then remembered that Cecily Foyle was coming round. She went to the door.

'Come on in,' said Faye.

Cecily was a tall elegant woman of Faye's own age. She and Faye had been students together, but Cecily had married young and had given up her work. When her marriage failed, leaving her with two sons, she had not gone back to Social work, but had taken a well paid job as an antique buyer for one of the big London stores. When Faye, purely by chance, had met her again, two years ago, they had at once renewed their friendship. Cecily was now alone; both her sons had grown up: Faye had suggested that she should recommend her as a Prison Visitor. Her hours of work were fluid, and she had a sympathetic and engaging personality. It was about her prison visiting that Cecily had in fact wanted to see her.

'Sure this isn't a bother?' said Cecily.

'Not a bit. I'd been going to ring you while Bill was away and suggest doing a theatre together.' She was pouring a drink as she spoke.

'Is he still as busy as ever?'

'Busier. For the past month he's been commuting between Basle and Beirut.'

'What does he do, actually?' asked Cecily.

'Advises people where and what to build.'

Cecily laughed. 'I can't, somehow, imagine Bill as a business tycoon with ulcers.'

'Neither can I. And mercifully he hasn't. When did you last see him?'

'All those years ago. When he looked very like that.' And Cecily pointed to a photograph of Paul on his boat. 'That's your son I presume?'

'You're right. He is like Bill used to be.'

'He's good looking. What's he doing now?'

'He's in Bangladesh. He got a goodish degree and then took a job with the Red Cross, doing community work, which is odd.'

'Why?'

'He used to despise the social services when he lived at home. But now he seems involved.'

Cecily laughed. 'It must run in the blood,' she said. 'I'd like to see Bill again.'

'You will if you stay on for a bit. He'll be back quite soon. He's flying home from Basle.'

'Good,' said Cecily. 'Then I'd better say what I came to say before he arrives. It's something – well – something serious. I want to talk to you.'

'Talk away,' said Faye: and thought what an attractive person Cecily was with her eyes which crinkled up as she smiled. Faye could not imagine why she had never got married again. Presumably because she hadn't wanted to risk it. Faye had gathered that her husband had been an extremely unpleasant character.

Cecily was not smiling for once.

'It's about my visiting, Stone Park I mean, not you.'

'What about it?'

'I feel I haven't exactly been a raving success.'

'Why?'

Cecily frowned. 'We-ll – I'm not particularly practical and I'm certainly not a great reformer.'

Faye smiled. 'If I thought you were going to start telling the women how to lead better lives I'd never have suggested your visiting.'

'Seriously?'

'Very seriously. I asked you to come because you make people laugh.'

'Oh.' Cecily was nonplussed. 'Thanks,' she said dryly.

Faye laughed. 'Don't be offended, you silly creature. We've got plenty of holier-than-thous wanting to visit. You are such a relief because you don't expect too much.'

'I don't expect anything except a good deal of foul language. Somethimes I even swear back.'

'And as a result you get more from them than the most fervent social lecturer. I expect you realise that I've given you some of the toughest ones as well as the most inarticulate and inverted.'

Cecily nodded. 'The thought had crossed my mind . . . so you think I'm doing all right?'

'I'd have told you pretty quickly if I hadn't.'

'You sound just like Mrs Armitage.'

'Cecily! How dare you.' And they both laughed.

After a pause Cecily said, 'I'm surprised. I try never to lecture them, I just rabbit on in my usual fluffy way about cooking, or clothes, or the telly, until they start talking themselves. And when they do,' she whistled. 'My goodness some of their stories are pretty hair raising.'

Faye gave her some more sherry. 'I don't mind betting you had one failure.'

'Who's that?'

'Lily Hever.'

Cecily frowned. 'I'm so bad at names. It's my tiny brain.

Oh, her, the woman under Rule 43. You're right. I had a go last time she was out – couldn't get near her. She called me "madam" every other sentence and underneath her politeness she was being just about as bitchy as could be.'

'Never mind,' said Faye. 'You can have another go next week.'

'Why? Is she coming out again?'

'She doesn't want to but I'm insisting that she does. The staff, none of them, agree with me.'

'I don't think I do either,' said Cecily.

'I'm convinced that it would be irresponsible to leave Lily alone in her cell any longer. I've read too many reports of the effects that total isolation can have on prisoners. So, if the staff don't like it they must lump it. Lily will come out tomorrow.'

'And look out for squalls,' thought Cecily. But she didn't say so. Her friend was wearing her official face, and when she did that, it was better not to disagree with her. Instead she said. 'Now Vivien Pearce. There's a different kettle of fish.'

Faye smiled, 'I gave you Vivien as a bonus. I knew she'd be a relief after some of the others. I'm relying on you to drive her when she goes for her home visit in a few weeks.'

'Good. I'd like to meet her mum. Vivien's devoted to both her parents. They sound a jolly family. How on earth did she land up inside?'

'The old story,' said Faye. 'She became involved with the wrong man. One of the Stern brothers.'

Again Cecily whistled. 'Whew! Which one?'

'Max Stern.'

'Golly golly gumdrops.' (One of Cecily's more endearing habits was that of using expressions she had caught from her schoolboy brothers some forty years ago.) 'Isn't he the one who got ten years for dope smuggling just lately?'

'Yes.'

'But surely Vivien wasn't involved in that?'

'She wasn't involved in anything in my opinion. Some stolen jewels were found hidden in her flat. She swore she knew nothing about them.'

'I don't suppose the police believed a word of that.'

'I think they might have. Vivien had absolutely no record and came from a very respectable middleclass background, only—'

Faye paused and shrugged her shoulders.

'Only, what?'

'She absolutely refused to implicate anyone else in the matter, so the police were obliged to arrest her.'

' "Sacrificing herself for her loved one",' said Cecily. 'Can't say I blame her. Did you see his photographs? He's wildly attractive.'

'Maybe.' Faye's voice was rather cold. 'A lot of villains are. But he did his best to ruin the girl's life. Fortunately he's not succeeded.'

'I'd say not. She's neither inverted nor bitter.'

'No. Though I can't imagine why she isn't. Because, as it turns out, she sacrificed herself for nothing.'

'Exactly,' said Cecily.

'I went to see her myself when Stern was sent down. And I swear that it was a complete shock to her. I'm sure she had no idea he was involved in high crime.'

'Does she still love him, d'you think?'

'It's not easy to find out what Vivien is thinking. But I'd say not.'

'Good. Then she'll be able to start again when she comes out.'

'Yes,' said Faye. 'She will.'

She rose.

'I must go and fiddle about in the kitchen. Give yourself a drink. I'll switch on the telly.'

Cecily poured herself a drink and sat down, very much at peace with the world. She had been worried before she had talked to Faye. She had been afraid that she was not sufficiently professional in her approach. But now she felt reassured, glad to know that her work as a prison visitor had won official approval.

From the kitchen came a clatter of dishes, as Faye busied herself with dinner. She was humming to herself tunelessly. Cecily smiled as she listened. Faye was so obviously happy at the thought of Bill's return.

The News came up on the television screen. The Queen was visiting a Commonwealth country, driving past flag waving children in the pouring rain: the Prime Minister, in a fur hat several sizes too large for him, had arrived in Moscow: a picket at a factory in the north had been severely injured by a flying pick. Cecily giggled. Had the newsreader really said 'a flying pig'? And then suddenly she was serious again and alert. The regular news had been interrupted by a 'flash' and the newsreader's voice had taken on a suitably urgent tone.

'News is just coming in of a hijacking at Basle Airport. A Swissair Caravelle, flight number SR 102, due to leave for London at 17.15 was seized by gunmen as it was taxi-ing to the end of the runway for take off. . . .'

Cecily got up. Faye was still clattering in the kitchen section of the room and obviously had not heard. She must be told. Cecily could only pray that Bill had not caught that particular plane. The newsreader was still speaking:

'It is still not known who the hijackers are nor what are their objectives. But it is believed that the aircraft was carrying a full load of passengers, among them many Britons. As soon as we have any further news, we will bring it to you.'

The newsreader paused, then continued in a different tone:

'And now – here is a preview of next spring's fashions. . . .'

Cecily turned down the sound and went to join Faye, who was putting a casserole into the oven. She looked up at Cecily and smiled.

'One of Bill's favourite things,' she said.

Then she saw Cecily's face and asked quickly.

'What is it?'

'There's been a newsflash. A flight from Basle. . . .'

'Which one?'

'Quarter past five to London.'

Faye straightened up. Every vestige of colour had left her face. When she spoke her voice was barely audible.

'It's crashed!'

'No, not as bad as that. It's a hijack.'

Cecily hoped she did not sound as shaky as she felt. She saw that Faye's hands were trembling.

'I'm going to give you some of your own brandy,' she said and led Faye into the living room.

She poured her a stiff drink, then switched the television over to the other channel, hoping they might have more detailed news. They had. She and Faye listened in silence.

The hijackers, three in number, had announced themselves as members of 'The Scourge' – a breakaway group of fanatical Arab terrorists, who had been repudiated by more orthodox Palestinian organisations. They were demanding the release of two of their fellows, currently held in Switzerland, pending extradition to France on charges of murder and sabotage. They had given a deadline of 11.00 pm for the Swiss Government to comply with their demand. After that they threatened to start shooting hostages. The news item ended with a warning that the airline did not have a complete list of passengers, and gave a number for friends and relatives to ring.

Faye switched off. She was very controlled.

'Bill was only *hoping* to catch that flight,' she said. 'We must find out if he actually went on board before we start worrying too much.'

But in her heart of hearts she felt sure that he must be on the plane. If not, surely he would have rung her from Basle when the news first broke? Or had he been trying and was there a long delay on calls?

Meanwhile she threw Cecily a book in which she had listed the various hotels at which Bill usually stayed and asked her to ring the Basle hotel, while she herself rang the Heathrow number quoted on television.

After a frustrating delay, Faye finally got through. They were sympathetic but could not confirm or deny that Mr Boswell was a passenger. Nor could they give her any further news, but took her number and promised to ring her, if they had any.

On the other line Cecily was still waiting for her Basle connection. Faye thought for a moment, then rang a friend on the editorial staff of BBC News. He too was full of sympathy and gave her all the information he had, but it was very little more than had already been broadcast.

By this time Cecily had got her number. Faye's heart sank. Evidently there was no undue delay on calls between London and Basle. If Bill had missed the plane, he could have rung her by now.

Cecily was speaking to the Porter (fount of all knowledge in a good hotel). He confirmed that Mr Boswell had been staying there but had checked out in plenty of time to catch the 17.15 flight.

'So he is on it,' said Faye, and even Cecily could find no words of hope.

There was a moment's silence. As a drowning man's whole life is said to pass before his eyes, so Faye saw her future as it would be, if Bill did not return.

The silence was broken by the telephone ringing. It was Peter Mayes, who knew that Bill was due back from Basle on that flight. He was coming round, he said, and it was useless for Faye to try and stop him. She did not try – did not want to.

The evening wore on. There was no further news at nine o'clock nor at ten o'clock; and both reports were comparatively brief. Hijackings are commonplace nowadays and do not merit special treatment, unless there is a Prime Minister or pop star on board.

Grateful for her two friends' company, Faye sat and waited for news that did not come, while the Caravelle sat on the runway and hijackers and hostages alike also waited – as time moved on to the deadline.

Eleven o'clock came and went. Faye still managed to keep herself under control, but inwardly she was beginning to panic. Peter Mayes tried to reassure her. No doubt negotiations were still continuing. Deadlines were always extended.

But he was wrong. It came through on News Extra. Two passengers, both men, but still unidentified, had been shot; their bodies had been thrown out of the plane and were lying on the runway.

For the next hour or so Faye rang, in a kind of fever, anyone whom she thought might have news. Bill's partner; a friend at Scotland Yard; an acquaintance at Reuters. Everyone was kind and sympathetic but no-one had any information about the identity of the dead hostages and no-one knew any more details of the negotiations between the hijackers and the Swiss authorities. By now the television services had closed down and they were relying on London Broadcasting which gave news bulletins through the night.

At one o'clock Peter Mayes suggested that some food would do them all good and Cecily produced an excellent omelette. Faye insisted that she couldn't touch a thing, but she found to her amazement that she ate her share with a sharp appetite.

Cecily fought back a yawn. She had had a long day. At Faye's suggestion she went up to sleep in Paul's bedroom. Peter Mayes and Faye talked into the small hours. At first, anxiously, about the hijacking and then inevitably about Stone Park, and the many problems there. After discussing various difficult inmates they turned to more general matters, and

Faye confessed to the doctor that, despite the reforms she had managed to achieve, she was afraid that prison had not changed appreciably since the early years of this century. In detail, yes, but the basic concept had remained the same.

'When I went to Stone Park,' Faye admitted, 'I was full of reforming zeal. Too full perhaps. I saw a few too many stars. But now – it's depressing, but I begin to see the Chief's point of view more clearly.'

'I think you underrate yourself, Faye. You've achieved a great deal. Be honest and admit it.' He got up and looked down at her. 'Are you going to work tomorrow?'

'Of course.'

'I thought that would be your answer. So I want you to go upstairs, take this sleeping pill and a hot drink, and get three or four hours sleep. In fact as your doctor I order you.'

'You're not my doctor.' But Faye's protest was only half-hearted.

Peter Mayes came back from the kitchen with the hot drink.

'Take this and then up you go . . . I don't want to be depressing but this state of suspense could go on for days. If you don't sleep you'll be fit for nothing, and when Bill gets back he'll have our blood for not looking after you.'

Faye smiled at him. She rose and put her hand on his shoulder. What a nice man he was, although his deliberate optimism did not for a moment fool her.

'Bless you Peter,' she said. Aren't you going home now?'

'I'll snatch forty winks on your sofa. I'll go home later for a bath and shave. I'd rather stay here for the moment.'

He did not add 'in case the news came through that Bill had been one of the hostages who were shot.' But she knew he was thinking it and he knew she knew. She went upstairs obediently, thinking she would lie awake till morning. But instead she fell asleep almost at once and slept dreamlessly for three hours.

CHAPTER FIVE

Faye did not wake till well after seven, and lay drowsily for a few contented moments, not fully awake. Then the sound of the wireless downstairs woke her more thoroughly and the whole story came flooding back into her mind. She put on her dressing gown and went downstairs.

She had a headache, she was not used to sleeping pills. A comforting clatter came from the kitchen together with one of the best smells in the world – that of freshly ground coffee.

Cecily was busy in the kitchen. She was not yet dressed. She had borrowed a dressing gown of Paul's from her room; and looked, with her curly short hair and elegant body, remarkably like an ageing boy herself.

She smiled when she saw Faye, who looked quite unlike her normal self.

'Drink this,' and put a steaming mug of coffee in front of her. Faye sipped it thankfully.

'Any news?' she asked automatically.

'Yes,' said Cecily. 'Good news, at least for you, not for them, the two dead hostages, I mean. One was Swiss and the other was German.'

'Thank God,' said Faye. 'Anything else?'

'It looks as if the Swiss authorities are going to give way. At any rate they've taken the two prisoners to the Airport. But one of those know-all commentators said they might still be playing for time.'

'What's the time now?' asked Faye.

'Getting on for half past seven.'

'Has Peter gone?'

'Yes. He waited to hear the news at six o'clock and then went off for a bath and a shave. He said not to worry, any doctor can do without sleep – and anyhow he said your Habitat sofa is more comfortable than most beds.'

'I'm very lucky in my friends,' said Faye, which sounded like a non sequitur. But Cecily understood. She patted Faye's hand and said. 'We were both glad to be with you.'

Faye pushed her mug forward. 'I could do with some more of that,' she said. 'I'm feeling a bit groggy. Have I time for a long bath? I must set my hair too.' For she did not intend to arrive at the Home Office looking less than her immaculate self.

'Of course you have. What time do you have to be at Stone Park?'

'I'm not going there. I've got a meeting at the Home Office, Departmental Planning. It's not till half past ten. I arranged with Charles yesterday for him to take Duties and do the rounds for me today.' She paused. 'It's a bit odd that he didn't ring up.'

'I expect he was out last evening.'

As though on cue the telephone rang.

'I'll take it,' said Cecily quickly, for she saw that Faye was dreading bad news. But it was only Charles. She handed the telephone to Faye.

'It's your Deputy,' she said.

'Faye?' said Charles. 'I've only just heard about that plane. It wasn't, by any awful chance. . . .'

He didn't have time to finish his sentence. Faye's voice came back to him.

'Yes. I'm afraid it is. No news at all . . . one can only hope.' Her voice sounded shaky.

'I feel a brute. I'd have rung you last night, only we went out. Have you been alone?'

'Far from it. Don't worry Charles. I've had two very good friends with me.' Her voice changed, became more authoritative, calmer.

'You know I'm not coming in this morning? I'll go straight

to the Home Office. The Development Committee is meeting and I must put forward our case for those short term improvements we discussed.'

'Are you certain you're fit to go?'

'Positive. But I'd like you to have a word with that woman on remand, Chatterton. She's in some sort of worry over her solicitor, and her case comes into court in a day or two. If necessary get on to Prisoners' Aid.'

'I'll do that thing.'

'Good. And see that the Works Manager gets the hot pipes in South Wing recess attended to. He's been very dilatory over it and Martha Parrish is going to lose her temper soon.'

'Right.'

'Then I'll see you after lunch. Goodbye. And thank you for ringing,' said Faye crisply, with a faint touch of sarcasm in her voice.

She rang off and got up.

'Now for that bath,' she said to Cecily. 'Thank heaven I've a bit more time than usual. I need it to make myself presentable.' And she added as she got to the door. 'My faithful Mrs Burton will be back today, thank goodness. She's been away whilst her daughter was in hospital. So you can just leave everything. She hates it if one does her work for her.'

Cecily had watched Faye, amazed, as she talked to Charles. Was this the tired bedraggled woman who had come drifting in half an hour ago? She had been transformed into the Governor under Cecily's eyes. There was something to be said for the discipline of work.

Charles Radley rang off, somewhat nonplussed. In an odd sort of way, he felt snubbed. He had rung up expecting to offer a shoulder to weep on, and instead found himself being given some brisk orders. He smiled ruefully. He knew how much Faye relied on him, and guessed that she had missed him last evening. He must explain when he saw her later in the day. Better not now, in case Beth heard. Women were funny creatures, and could not understand that one could be deeply involved with the colleague one worked with so closely, without necessarily being interested in her as a woman.

Beth appeared at the door.

'Was it Bill's plane?'

'Yes.'

'What hell for her. How did she sound?'

'Her usual brisk self,' said Charles, rather dryly. 'I've got to be in early this morning, so I'll be off. You're going to the Clinic aren't you? Take care of yourself. I'll ring if I'm going to be home late.' And he kissed her and left.

Soon after nine Faye reappeared, looking her usual self. She had made up carefully and the dark lines under her eyes were hidden.

Cecily was attacking a large breakfast. She was one of those women who could eat enormously and still keep her willowy figure. Faye toyed with a piece of toast and drank more coffee.

'Headache better?'

'Much.'

'Peter Mayes left a note.' She passed it to Faye, who read it and smiled briefly.

'He wants you to drive me today.'

'D'you mind?'

'I'm delighted. I'd like your company. We needn't leave for a bit. What about ringing up to ask Heathrow if they've any news?'

'I have, and they haven't.'

'I see,' said Faye. Cecily noticed that there was a tiny pulse at the corner of her mouth which was twitching. In every other way she was in complete control.

As they had time to spare before leaving for the Home

Office, Faye insisted on turning on the wireless, although Cecily tried to dissuade her.

'Try to understand,' Faye said, 'I must know what's happening. It's going to be bad enough sitting through that Committee this morning; at least I can listen now. Besides it may be good news.'

It was not good news. It was the most disturbing news they had yet had.

At half past nine the terrorists, evidently suspecting some move by the troops surrounding the airport, began firing at them. Almost immediately the troops returned the fire. The exchange of fire did not last long, but long enough for two soldiers and several of the passengers in the plane to be wounded.

For a while nothing more happened, then the negotiators managed to arrange a truce for the wounded to be removed.

Boarding steps had been sent out and stretchers for the more severe cases. But the hijackers would allow nobody to go on board; so a steward, himself slightly wounded, and one of the passengers, believed to be a doctor, came off with the wounded, and acted as stretcher bearers, carrying the badly injured to the waiting ambulances. The total number of injured was fifteen. Five were seriously hurt; and the rest were being flown home after medical attention.

At the moment everything was quiet again. But the hijackers had reiterated their demands. The two arrested terrorists were to be released: and another aircraft (not riddled with bullet holes) was to stand by, ready to fly to the Near East. Failing compliance, they would blow up the Caravelle and everyone in it, including themselves: and the deadline for this ultimatum was 2.00 pm, Swiss time, or one o'clock, London time.

There was a moment's stunned pause. Then Faye turned to Cecily. 'If I take a taxi to the Home Office, will you get the names of the wounded? Dozens of people will be trying to get through, but when you find out, ring me at this extension at the Home Office. It's the office of a friend of mine who'll be at the same Committee meeting. Simply say, "Bill isn't wounded – or he is".'

She paused, then added as she rang a taxi:

'Can you imagine? Here I am praying that Bill is wounded, simply to know that he's safely off that plane.'

Before they left Faye wrote a note to Mrs Burton and put the telephone on transfer, so that all calls on the private line were automatically referred to her office at Stone Park. She also rang Penny to put her in the picture, and to tell her to send any urgent calls through to the secretary of one of her friends at the Home Office, who could then contact her.

'Yes of course,' said Penny. She was businesslike and brisk and tactfully did not offer Faye her sympathy, for which Faye was thankful. Until she knew what had happened to Bill, she must carry on. That meant keeping an iron grip on herself: and if people were going to sympathize, this was something she could not do.

At the committee meeting, Faye sat next to her friend, Mrs Headley. Faye knew her well, in fact she had been Deputy Governor at Stone Park, before Faye went there. She was now at the Home Office as an Assistant Director of Prisons. She had been told the news about Bill Boswell, and was slightly surprised to find that Faye had come to the meeting; though, knowing Faye to be a woman of integrity and strength, she could understand why she had done so.

As it turned out, Faye need perhaps not have bothered. She had come to stress the importance of making some short term structural improvements which she knew were urgently needed at Stone Park. But before the meeting started, the Chairman read out a memorandum from the Treasury, which made it clear that, in the present financial climate, no funds could be made available for improvements to the existing prison; although the new prison which was rising round the original one would continue to be built and be ready for occupation in some five years time.

'So that's that,' thought Faye, and wondered whether she would, after all, read the paper which she had prepared. She glanced at the Agenda. Her name was on it. She must make her speech. It would do no harm. Who knows, it might even do some good?

Just before it was her turn to speak, she said to Mrs Headley:

'There may be a message for me via your secretary. She'll bring it to you. It's personal. All right?'

Mrs Headley who knew perfectly well what it was about put her hand over Faye's and murmured:

'Perfectly all right, my dear,' and added, 'Good luck.'

And Faye knew this did not refer to the statement she was going to make.

She managed to speak with authority and conviction, and her prepared jokes went down well. She did not even falter when a messenger came into the room and gave a piece of paper to Mrs Headley.

When she sat down there was a little murmur of approbation. She did not notice, but turned to Mrs Headley, who handed her the paper with a sympathetic look. As she opened it, her heart was beating faster than usual.

'A message for Mrs Boswell,' she read. 'Mr Boswell is not among the wounded.'

The room span round Faye, as she realised the implications of this. Bill was still on the plane – the plane which might be blown up within a few hours. She gripped the side of her chair tightly to steady herself.

'Can you cope?' asked Mrs Headley quietly.

Faye nodded.

'If not, we'll all understand. But that statement of yours

made a very good impression; and if you could bear to stay and answer some questions, I think you've a fair chance of getting some of what you want, despite the Treasury memorandum.'

Faye was amazed to hear this. As far as she was concerned, she might have been reciting the Lord's Prayer backwards instead of making a reasoned speech. With a superhuman effort she put Bill out of her mind and set herself to answering the questions which the committee members put to her.

At the end of the meeting she was looking, through she did not know it, utterly drained. Mrs Headley offered her both lunch and a drink. She accepted the latter and refused the former. They did not talk about Bill; indeed Faye was not conscious that they talked at all.

Mrs Headley insisted on going down to the door with her, to make certain her friend had arrived to drive her home – not to the prison. She felt that, until she knew whether she was wife or widow, it would be better for the Governor to leave Stone Park to her deputy.

Cecily's little blue mini was near the entrance, illegally parked. A warden was approaching as rapidly as his bulk permitted.

'Hurry,' said Mrs Headley, 'or he'll get her.'

She and Faye went quickly down the steps to the car which Cecily had now moved to the entrance. Faye got in and Mrs Headley went round and spoke softly to Cecily.

'Take her home,' she said. 'I'll ring up and have a word with the Deputy. Perhaps you could get in touch with her doctor?'

'I'll do that,' said Cecily, and drove away under the very nose of the warden, who stood looking after her, book in hand, thwarted of his prey.

Mrs Headley went back to her room and switched on her radio hoping for more news. The hijack story had gained momentum, because the media sensed disaster and were giving it plenty of coverage. But at the moment there was nothing fresh. Mrs Headley picked up the telephone and asked for the Deputy Governor of Stone Park prison.

At Stone Park, several of Faye's colleagues were also anxious for news. When Mrs Headley's call came through, Charles Radley, Peter Mayes and Janet Harker were in the Deputy's room, waiting for the lunchtime bulletin on the small portable television which Janet had had the foresight to bring along with her.

Charles finished talking to Mrs Headley, rang off and looked at the expectant faces.

'Bill isn't among the wounded,' he said briefly. 'Faye got a message during the meeting.'

'She shouldn't have gone,' said Janet indignantly.

'She insisted on going,' answered Peter Mayes. 'It was the Reconstruction and Development Committee.'

'Wasted effort,' said Charles Radley. 'I don't mind betting the Treasury won't cough up just now.'

As it happened he was wrong. But no one was to know that until some months later.

Just then the lunchtime news came on and Janet flew to the sound and turned it up.

A correspondent was reporting from Basle. Far away in the distance could be seen the grounded plane. He was speaking in the rather excited urgent voice which viewers know too well, as it is always used when the news is grim (which is nowadays practically weekly).

'I am speaking to you from Basle Airport,' he was saying, 'where the atmosphere is now very tense indeed. As you can see, the troops have been withdrawn to the perimeter of the airfield; and it appears that all efforts at conciliation have failed. It seems that this is the moment of truth.'

* * *

Cecily had no wireless in her car, and Faye was urging her to drive faster, in order to catch the news at home.

'You can easily do it in half an hour,' she said. 'I always do.'

'Perhaps you're a better driver than I am,' thought Cecily, as she forced her mini through the traffic, earning curses from bus and taxi drivers and nearly running down some harmless pedestrians, in her effort to do as Faye wanted.

During the journey Faye sat quite rigid, hardly moving or speaking. At five minutes to one the car drew up outside the Boswells' house. Faye bolted inside, and Cecily followed. The few seconds while the set warmed up seemed interminable. Then he was there – out man in Basle, good looking, young, brown faced, wearing an expensive looking sheepskin coat. They had missed the opening of the news, and he was just saying, 'It seems that this is the moment of truth.'

He looked at his watch, then continued:

'It is now coming up to two o'clock Swiss time, which is the terrorists' deadline. A few minutes ago a message was delivered to the hijackers, and it is believed that it carries a refusal to accede to their demands. The question we are all asking now is, will they carry out their threat and destroy not only themselves and the aircraft, but forty innocent passengers as well?'

'Don't watch any more,' said Cecily suddenly, urgently, moving towards the set.

'Leave it!' Faye's voice was anguished.

The atmosphere in the room was thick with tension. Both women were staring at the screen, waiting to see God knows what horror.

Then, abruptly, without warning, the door opened. They turned, as Bill came in. Faye stood up. Her face was ashen.

'Bill . . .' she sighed and folded neatly on to the floor.

* * *

Later, Faye was lying in bed, drowsy and near to sleep. Her doctor had been and ordered her to bed for the afternoon. He had also given her a sedative, for she was in a state of mild shock.

Cecily, having fed Bill, had gone, with profuse thanks from both the Boswells and profuse apologies from Faye; for Faye was horrified at her own behaviour. She had never fainted in her life before today. But now, she told herself, she must talk to Bill. Before she slept, she must find out what had happened.

Bill put his hand, warm and dry and comforting, over hers, which was still trembling a little.

'I thought you were on the plane,' she said.

'Poor old love. You must have been through merry hell.'

'Please explain what happened.' Her voice was still shaking.

'When the wounded were allowed to go off, someone had to go with them, as the ambulance men weren't allowed near the plane, and some of them were stretcher cases – including one child whose leg was smashed up.'

'Oh Bill, how horrible!'

'It wasn't nice. I was sitting near the door, so I got myself the job of stretcher bearer, with one of the stewards who'd been slightly hurt. After we'd heaved down the stretchers and helped the others out and carried down the child, I got into one of the ambulances with them.'

'The news said something about a doctor.'

'That was reporters jumping to conclusions. When we got to the hospital, we were besieged by the press. The doctors got rid of them by promising a list of names of the wounded and interviews with the less severe cases. No one asked my name and, like a fool, I never gave it. I was too busy finding out about planes home.'

'You might have rung me.'

'I tried to, but there wasn't a free line. So I gave this

number to a girl at the Swissair Office, I paid for the call and slipped her an extra ten francs. She got through half an hour ago, while the doctor was with you. Of course I'd have kept on trying myself, only they'd just told me I might catch a London flight from Zurich, if I could find a taxi driver who could get me there in under two hours. It was quite a drive and it cost me a fortune, but we made it.'

Faye sighed. Sleep was beginning to overcome her. Then she remembered and there was still a tremor in her voice, when she spoke.

'And the plane? The other passengers?'

'Still there; but they won't be much longer.'

'We thought they were going to blow it up.'

'So did everyone. The final negotiations were kept secret for some reason. Possibly because the French Government was involved and might have wanted to take a tougher line.'

'The Swiss have given them what they wanted?'

'What else could they do? Two people had been killed already and several more wounded. They couldn't risk the lives of another forty. They're handing over the two prisoners, supplying another plane and a fresh crew – and a member of the Government as hostage. They should be taking off any minute now. Then those other poor devils – my fellow passengers, I mean – will be free.'

'How do you know all this?'

'It came through later on the news – the same news you were watching when I came in. You'd have seen it yourself, if you hadn't chosen to faint. It may have been my imagination but I thought the reporter looked faintly disappointed when the Caravelle didn't go up in smoke.'

Faye yawned, then took Bill's hand again.

'Darling, it must have been an appalling night.'

'It was. A baby that cried incessantly and one poor old woman had colly-wobbles. Most people behaved extremely well.'

'And the hijackers?'

'They behaved like human beings too most of the time – which is extraordinary, as they must in fact be quite inhuman to do what they did.'

'They did send the wounded off.'

Bill laughed shortly.

'That was only because one was screaming and another was bleeding rather badly. One of the boys – all the hijackers were pretty young, but this one couldn't have been more than sixteen – wanted to go round administering the coup-de-grace. He was the one who'd started the shooting – very trigger happy indeed. So the man in charge knocked him out with a pistol butt. He may even have killed him for all I know – or care.'

Faye spoke very sleepily:

'That type – we have some of them, you know – at Stone Park. They don't spare anyone – don't spare themselves either. We live in a barbaric world, darling.'

Her voice tailed off; her eyes shut; the sedative was taking effect. Bill bent over and kissed the top of her head.

'Sleep now,' he said.

Later he would sleep himself, but first he must ring Stone Park and tell Charles Radley that Faye would not be back this afternoon.

CHAPTER SIX

In the staff room at Stone Park a post mortem was taking place. All the staff had been stirred by the hijacking, for the news that 'Madam's' husband was one of the passengers had quickly travelled round the prison. Most of them were kindly women at heart and would no doubt have been horrified if they had realised that they had been pleasantly excited by the possibility that Mr Boswell might have been blown up.

'Under his wife's very eyes, so to speak,' said Miss Dudgeon excitedly.

Miss Dudgeon was one of the Prison Officers, new to Stone Park. She was a blonde rather odd looking young woman with curly hair, who had, in Faye's opinion, a positive genius for saying the wrong thing and putting people's backs up, although strangely enough the inmates seemed to like her.

Mrs Armitage could not bear her, but since there were few people that she could bear this meant very little.

'You needn't sound so disappointed, Miss Dudgeon,' she now said, her Northern accent stronger than ever.

'Whatever do you mean – disappointed? Poor dear Mrs Boswell. What would she have done?'

'She'd have coped – and coped very well,' answered the Chief.

'Well,' thought Martha Parrish, who was as usual sitting listening and saying very little, 'listen to that! The Chief standing up for the Governor! What next?'

Miss Berryman stubbed out one of her inevitable cigarettes. She was a dark personable young woman, who had entered the prison service with high ambitions and hopes of rapid promotion. But although she had a vigourous personality and intense energy, she was unfortunately not a particularly disciplined person; she had a tendency to question orders, and had twice been reported for smoking on duty. Also, unlike some of the officers, she had a very active sex life.

'What about Lily Hever?' she asked the Chief. 'Is she to come out now, or are we to wait till Madam comes in?'

'She isn't coming. Her doctor's ordered her to rest,' said Mrs Armitage.

'Lucky old her!' said Dudgeon, in what the Chief thought was an impertinent way.

'Any news of her husband?' asked Berryman.

'Yes,' said the Chief briefly, 'he's back.' And to avoid any more talk about her Governor she added:

'We'd better get on with our work.'

Miss Parrish remained drinking her coffee and reflecting that the Governor had for once made a grave error of judgment. To bring Lily Hever back into association with the other inmates on her wing could only lead to trouble.

Mrs Armitage was thinking very much the same thing as she led the way to North Wing. She went into Janet Harker's office and shut the door.

Janet looked up, surprised.

'What is it Chief?' she asked.

'Fact is I'm worried,' said Mrs Armitage. And she looked it.

'Do sit down,' said Janet, and to her great surprise the Chief did so. She had something to say but seemed to find it difficult to begin.

'I . . .' she said, and hesitated. 'The fact is, Janet . . . it's about Fran Morris. Big Fran. And Lily. Madam has made a terrible mistake and I told her. I'd tell her again if she was here.'

'I don't think she'd listen,' said Janet.

'She wouldn't, not any road. So I was wondering if you and I had better have a word with Fran herself. She's so near to the end of her term, only four more weeks, and she's earned full remission. It would be a shame for her if she did anything to spoil it now. So maybe if we talked to her?'

'Let's do that thing,' said Janet. And Big Fran, who was enjoying an energetic game of table-tennis was called in. Wearing a striped T shirt and slacks, with her short cropped blonded hair, she looked like the leader of a women's football team. She towered over Janet Harker and looked down at the Chief. She listened quietly whilst they told her that Lily was coming out of her cell. Then she said:

'Don't worry. I won't touch her, whatever she does. She's not worth losing my remission for.'

'That's just the way we think,' said Janet.

'All the same,' added Fran, 'she's poison. I'm surprised Madam wants her out.'

The two other women glanced at each other. They could not do anything but agree with Fran. Mrs Armitage rose briskly.

'Thanks Fran,' she said. 'I know we can rely on you. Now go and finish your game.'

She went outside and posted her officers where she thought was strategic. Then she went to Lily's cell.

'You can come out now,' she said.

Lily peered out nervously. Some of the inmates were playing cards or Monopoly (a game which was extremely popular on the Wing). Others were reading, while some of the older inhabitants were gossiping.

Lily was relieved to see that there were several screws on duty – more than usual as she remembered it. Miss Harker stood at the door of her office and the Chief was very much in evidence. But where was the Governor? Funny she wasn't there. Lily felt a little hurt.

Nobody seemed interested in Lily. She noticed this, partly with relief, partly with disappointment. She had brought her mug with her and sidled up to the trolley. Without any comment and with the briefest of smiles Miss Flaxton filled it for her.

She looked round. Should she go back into her cell? That would be a bit of an anti-climax. She noticed that a young depressed-looking girl was sitting by herself on a bench. Lily had a weakness for young and frightened girls; they were good material for her particular machinations. She went up to Sandra and sat next to her.

'New, aren't you?' she said.

Sandra looked up, surprised, then nodded.

'Thought so,' said Lily. 'What's your name?'

'Sandra. I was in K Block,' answered the girl.

Lily was instantly sympathetic.

'Got a kid then?'

Sandra nodded.

'Take it away, did they?'

Tears came into Sandra's eyes and she sniffed.

'Poor luv,' said Lily. 'Bloody rotten, they are. You better write to your MP.'

Sandra shook her head. 'You don't understand. I asked them to put him in care. This place upsets him.'

Out of the corner of her eye Lily saw Mrs Armitage looking at her. She was also aware that Miss Berryman had muttered something about her to Janet Harker. 'Those bleeding screws,' she thought. 'Still, better play it cool.'

'We'll have another talk, eh?' she said softly to Sandra. 'Must go now.'

She got up and meandered round the wing; she looked in on old Lizzie who gave her a very cold reception; she wandered out again and took up a good position near the television set, shortly to be switched on, to the annoyance of Reba who had hoped to get that particular chair.

Well, she was out. And it wasn't as bad as she'd feared.

Maybe those other animals weren't going for her after all. And that new kid, Sandra, she looked easy enough.

Mrs Armitage left the wing. On the stairs she ran into Vivien who had been helping in the library.

'Oh, Vivien,' she said, 'Lily Hever's out of her cell.'

'What a pity,' answered Vivien crisply.

The Chief, who was in complete agreement with her, was not going to take this from an inmate, even if she was a Redband.

'That's not for you to say. I just wanted you to warn Sandra not to believe much that Lily says. They were talking together.'

'I'll do that with pleasure,' said Vivien.

Vivien lay and listened to Sandra's meandering and somewhat boring chatter about her baby. She hoped that it would not be too long before the girl found another cell-mate. She wished that Janet Harker had not asked her to share. She did greatly value her privacy and now, temporarily, she had lost it.

Sandra's voice grew quieter and finally stopped. She was asleep. Vivien stretched herself out and lay, her hands behind her head, taking stock of her life. She must decide what to do with herself when she got out. Soon she would be going for her pre-release home visit; and soon after that she would be released.

Vivien had been brought up in a small country town, where her father was one of the local bank managers. She had always been on good terms with her parents, and had missed the more obvious teenage problems. She had done well at school and had then gone into the bank to please her father. She had become engaged to a young man who worked there. She was fond of him but their sex life had been strained and unsatisfactory. In a way it had been a relief when he had been promoted and moved to another town; and the relationship had died a natural death.

She had found her work in the bank boring and repetitive. She longed for a wider horizon and, when she was twenty-one, she had left and gone to live in London, where she took a course in Beauty Counselling and later went to work in one of the big stores in the Cosmetics Department. By the time she was twenty-four she had become manageress of the department and her life had settled into a pleasant, if rather uneventful, routine. Only one thing worried her. She did not seem to be able to do more than *like* any of the men whom she met. She sometimes wondered if she was frigid.

It was three years since she had met Max. He had come into the store where she worked and had been instantly attracted to her; and, since he was a man who took what he wanted in life, he set about weakening her defences. It was not very difficult, for Vivien was as eagerly attracted to him as he was to her.

Max asked her out for a drink that evening, and the following night they dined, expensively and deliciously: it was the sort of meal and service that Vivien had read about but had never experienced. And, when the evening ended in bed in her flat, Vivien learnt that, whatever else she might be, she was not frigid.

For five months she lived a life of delicious sin. Max seemed to have unlimited money. He gave Vivien constant extravagant presents. Once he took her to Paris for a week-end and another time to Sardinia for a week. He was amusing and extrovert and an amazingly accomplished lover.

Vivien lived entirely for the present, never thinking of the future at all. But, looking back on it now, she could not imagine how she had not realised that Max was a 'villain'. His frequent absences, the fact that she was never told where he lived and had not even a telephone number for him: and there was that curious encounter with a tall good looking man, nearly as well dressed as Max himself, who had been in a bar one evening.

'Hullo, Max,' Vivien had heard him say. 'What are you doing on my manor?'

She did not hear Max's reply, as the two men drank at the bar together; and soon after that Max made an excuse to leave.

She remembered that she had wondered whether Max himself was a CID man. 'How green can you get?' she thought bitterly, lying on her narrow bed at Stone Park.

One day, in another bar, Max had been away telephoning. He seemed to spend half his life 'making a call' or 'contacting a fella'. Although he had told her that he ran a chain of garages in north London, he never seemed to keep office hours. On that particular day, his call had taken longer than usual. A girl with long dark hair had come into the bar and sat at a table near Vivien. She was looking towards the door. She had a fine boned profile and Vivien was admiring her beauty when she turned so that she was seen full face.

The right hand side of her face was cruelly scarred – slashed and puckered, the eye blinded. For a moment the girl looked full at Vivien, then she got up and left, her long dark wings of hair obscuring as much as possible of her grotesquely scarred face. For a moment Vivien felt physically sick. 'Poor poor girl,' she thought. 'What could have caused it? And why did she look at me in that strange way?' For the first time she felt out of her depth, frightened by some unknown menace.

Some instinct prevented her from mentioning the girl to Max; and that night she could not find her usual joy in their love making – though she managed to hide the fact from him.

About a week later, coming home with Max, she was waiting while he parked his car. A taxi drove past and slowed for a moment, without stopping; and in it Vivien thought she caught a glimpse of a white face with two long dark wings of hair. But she told herself she must have imagined it.

Max was in high spirits that night, opening champagne and laughing a lot, and then insisting on listening to the News. There was a report of a successful bank raid in Bloomsbury that morning, where the thieves got away with over £100,000.

'The police have a number of leads,' the newsreader was saying.

'Bless their little hearts,' said Max, who was slightly drunk, which was unlike him; and then he added with apparent inconsequence:

'Enjoy your day by the sea, love?'

That morning Max had insisted that she take the day off and spend it at Brighton with him. He had taken a room at a hotel for a few hours and had made love furiously. For the first time Vivien had felt like a whore and had not liked it.

Later that evening, in bed, curiosity at last prompted her to ask him if he knew the girl with the scarred face. The expression in his brown eyes, usually so flippant and amused, changed and his face hardened as he looked at her. She felt suddenly that she was with a stranger.

'Yes,' he said, 'I know her. Annie. Very sad. But lovely girls must learn not to tell tales out of school, mustn't they?'

His strong flexible fingers were round her throat. The gesture was deliberate. 'I wouldn't want anything like that to happen to you. That pretty face of yours. So you'll be very careful, won't you, my beautiful Viv.'

After that, although she still shivered with anticipation whenever he took her, she also shivered with fright. It was a question of perfect fear casting out love. For now she knew that he was no ordinary business man but a highly successful and ruthless criminal.

The strain of hiding her feelings from him had been intense; and for that reason it was almost a relief when one evening, soon after her return from work, the door bell rang and two well dressed men asked her if she could spare a few minutes. They added very politely that they had a Search Warrant with them.

The few minutes stretched to an hour, as the two detectives searched the flat, while Vivien sat rigid, with a policewoman as chaperone. 'What were they looking for?' she wondered, 'And where would they find it?'

It was only a small flat – the first floor of a converted Victorian house – and if Max had hidden anything, there were not many hiding places. Then she remembered the boxroom, which was a cupboard on the landing where she kept her suitcases. It was locked, and the yale key was on the key ring in her bag. She remembered now that one night there had been a longer delay than usual before Max had driven away in his car after leaving her. Had he really put something there? And if so, what? A suitcase full of notes perhaps? And should she tell the police about the boxroom? No, she decided, not unless they asked.

Not being complete fools, they did ask: and she had to produce the key. They searched the cupboard and found what they were looking for – a small bag containing diamonds which, it later transpired, were the proceeds of a burglary at Hatton Garden, and were valued at £200,000.

Vivien was formally 'invited' to go with the detectives to the Police Station. She was advised politely to pack an overnight case, and she did so, watched by the serious looking young policewoman.

On arrival at the station, the questioning began. It was gently done at first, for the police had a shrewd suspicion that Vivien had known nothing of the actual burglary and were only waiting for a lead. But when she continued to deny that she had ever known Max Stern or to implicate him in any way, their exasperation began to grow and the iron hand began to show through the velvet glove.

The small room in which they were questioning her was lit by a strong striplight and Vivien soon had a blinding headache. Over and over again she had been tempted to give in, to cry out, 'I do know Max Stern; he is my lover; he has been constantly to my flat; please stop asking me questions and let me rest.' But, each time, Vivien had seen, as plainly as though the girl had been in the room with them, the crude scarred face of poor Annie, and behind the barrage of questions she had heard the voice of Max saying, 'So you'll be very careful, my beautiful Viv.'

During the evening another detective had come in, to listen to the game of verbal ping pong which was being played across the bare table. It was the man she had seen in the bar with Max. If he recognised her, her case would be hopeless and Max would believe that she had betrayed him. She gripped the edge of the table and prayed not to faint. But fortunately for Vivien the man in question had not even noticed her in the crowded bar that evening three months ago.

She was struck by the likeness of these men to Max himself. They all shared a toughness, a ruthless quality under a surface smoothness of manner. The hunter and the hunted had a strong affinity.

By four o'clock she was quite rigid with exhaustion and strain; and when finally the barbed questions ceased and she was taken down to the cells for the night, she would gladly have given her soul for a long hot bath and a comfortable bed; but of course neither of these was forthcoming.

As she drifted into an uneasy and unrefreshing sleep, she wondered why Annie had done this to her. For it was undoubtedly the scarred girl who had followed Max to her flat that night and had later told the police. Indeed they had virtually admitted as much. They had called, they said, 'acting on information received.'

Then it dawned on Vivien that it was Max whom Annie had hoped to get at. She had never believed that Vivien would stand up to police questioning; she would be bound to implicate Max.

'But I did stand up to it,' thought Vivien. 'I'm tougher than you think.'

And a tiny inner voice answered her, 'Not tougher, just more frightened of Max.'

The next morning she had been charged with 'being in possession . . .', then taken to the Police Court where she was remanded for trial. The police would have agreed to bail – willingly, for Max might try to contact her – but she refused to ask for it. She had no desire to involve her parents in this, she said, and she could not possibly find the necessary surety herself. This is what she told the court. Actually she was longing to be somewhere where Max could not get hold of her; and where better than in prison?

The next day she went to the Remand Wing at Stone Park and remained there until her trial. Although she found the prison routine and food depressing, and many of the other inmates unbearable, she was determined to make the best of it and quickly became a favourite among most of the prison officers, if only because she never made extra trouble for them.

While she was on remand, she saw in the papers that a girl with a badly scarred face known as Annie Shaw had been reported missing and that the police were concerned for her safety; then later that she had been found drowned. Vivien shivered when she read this and was more than ever thankful that she was locked behind so many iron doors.

She was given a sentence of two years, a shorter one than she had expected. But her pleasant manner in court and the fact that she obviously knew little of the robbery itself told in her favour.

After conviction she had been returned to the North Wing at Stone Park; and one day, when she had been there for a month, her daily newspaper was not available when she went to collect it. She presumed that something was going to be cut out which the authorities did not want her to see. A certain amount of censoring still goes on, and once before she had been given a paper with items cut out.

Later that morning she was told to go immediately to the Governor's office. Probably she had been too bossy, she thought, on her way there. She must be more careful. She did not however get the reprimand which she expected. Instead, Mrs Boswell greeted her very kindly and told her to sit down. Vivien did so, somehow pleased to be in a properly furnished room again. For, even with Faye's large official desk and filing cabinets, this was more sitting room than office.

'I wanted to see you, Vivien,' the Governor had said, 'before you read your paper. There is an item in it which may be something of a shock to you.'

'What could it be?' thought Vivien. 'Not the parents. They were not the sort of people who made news.'

Aloud she said politely, 'Yes, Madam?'

'It's your . . .' Faye hesitated, then started again. 'It's Max Stern. He has been convicted of trafficking in heroin and sentenced to ten years. I thought it might be a shock to you. We all of us realise how loyal you were to him and how much you must have loved him.'

Vivien did not answer for a moment. As the Governor had said, it was indeed a tremendous shock, but not – as she had assumed – a shock of horror, rather one of joy. To know that Max was out of the way for nearly seven years – that she would have time to start a new life somewhere else! It was too much for her, and she burst into floods of tears – tears, if only Faye had known it, of overwhelming relief.

The Governor had been kindness itself. She had sent her secretary to make some coffee – real coffee such as Vivien had not drunk since she was admitted – and had talked to her sympathetically and wisely. Vivien had had a sudden longing to tell the truth about the ruthless man whom she had once loved so much and of whom she was now so terrified. But she decided not to. She had only a comparatively short time left to serve. Better leave it, and let them all think her a girl who had sacrificed her freedom for her lover.

The time had passed more quickly than she would have believed possible and now it was drawing towards the end, as, with full remission, she would only have to serve sixteen months.

And now Vivien lay in her bunk, still with her hands behind her head, reviewing the past, contemplating the future. Soon it would be time for her home visit. She would go to her parents, of course, and they would discuss what she should do. She had had her share of luxury living and would be thankful to settle for a quieter life.

It was late. The peephole on the door was lifted and a beady eye looked in. The night staff were doing their rounds. In the bunk below, Sandra was sleeping soundly.

Vivien looked up through the archaic barred windows of the cell. Beyond was a clear starry sky. The sounds of the outside world came in faintly. Soon she would be out in that world, free again and, what was more, free of her fear of Max.

She sighed, turned on her side, closed her eyes. At last Vivien slept, a deep refreshing sleep.

CHAPTER SEVEN

The evening after the hijacking, Bill Boswell took matters into his own hands, and, without consulting his wife, cancelled the usual alarm call; with the result that neither he nor Faye woke till after nine.

Faye did not arrive till eleven o'clock, and Charles Radley took Disciplinary and did the rounds. At the staff meeting she was profusely apologetic to her colleagues, who were vehement in saying that she need not have come in at all.

She was touched at the sympathy and compassion they showed her. Only Mrs Armitage said nothing.

To ease her obvious embarrassment, Faye asked her how Lily Hever was.

'She's out, madam,' said the Chief. 'Fortunately everything went quietly. Of course I had a word with Fran first.'

'Good,' said Faye.

'Do you think there is anything wrong with old Lizzie, Doctor?' Janet asked.

'Why? Do you?'

'She complains of indigestion such a lot. And sometimes her colour is bad. Of course she never gets out, poor old thing, except in the summer. She's too rheumaticky for exercise.'

'Exactly,' said Peter Mayes. 'Don't you worry, Janet. Let's see what this new medicine does. One mustn't confuse prison pallor with ill health.'

'No doctor,' said Janet meekly. But she privately thought that her fiancé would have been less casual in his approach.

When the three women went back to their offices, Charles Radley and the doctor stayed behind. Faye took the opportunity of thanking Peter for his help the night before last.

'I'm sorry I was a broken reed,' said Charles. 'As I told you

I didn't hear till the next morning. I was taking Beth out to celebrate.'

'Her birthday?' said Peter.

'No.' Charles was looking embarrassed for some reason. 'The fact is – she said I could tell you, but keep it to yourselves for the present – we're going to—'

But Faye didn't let him finish.

'Oh Charles how marvellous. I couldn't be more pleased.'

And Peter added:

'I can't imagine you as a proud father, Charles.'

'I can. Tell Beth how pleased I am,' said Faye. 'Why not come round for a meal one evening quite soon, you too Peter. I know Bill will be dying to tell you all his adventures now that we know the other passengers are safe.'

And so it was arranged.

When Lily first came out she played it very cool indeed, talking politely to any new inmates who did not know her story. But gradually, the news crept round. 'Avoid Lily Hever, she's poison.' And Lily's bitterness grew more venomous.

Only Vivien, who was now, to her delight, on Library duty, and Sandra, who lived in her own dream world, did not realise what was going on.

One morning Miss Clarke was trying without much success to talk to Lily Hever. Now Lily was out on the Wing, she wanted to discuss the future with her, but Lily was not in any mood to accept advice.

'You don't know what it's like in here miss. You leave everyday, sign out, go where you please. The pictures, have a drink with a fella. You can get on a train and just keep going. Never come back if you don't want to.'

'So can you in a few weeks,' said Miss Clarke. 'You will be free.'

'Free!' said Lily bitterly.

'You'll be signed out at the gate and then you can go where you please, just like me.'

'Just like you! With a few quid from you, a couple of bob from the Discharged Prisoners Aid, what do I do, where do I go? Some stinking dosshouse.'

'I'll find you somewhere to live.'

'So you can keep tabs on me? No bloody thanks.'

'At least let me find you a job, so that you can support yourself.'

'I'll support myself all right,' said Lily.

'You say that. But if you don't have somewhere to go, or a job, you know what will happen. You'll end up in here again.'

Lily smiled, a bitter twisted smile. 'Not this time. I'll be too smart for them. I'll keep on the move. One jump ahead, see?'

'You'd much better let me find you some work.'

Lily decided to change her tactics. A whine crept into her voice.

'I'm not well enough to work. I've been brutalised. You say I've paid my debt to society. What about society's debt to me? I'm going to collect it.'

'How do you propose to do that?'

'All them local authorities. And charities too. I'll let them know the way I've been treated in here. I want compensation. I'm going to live soft from now on. They can keep me.'

'That is pure fantasy Lily.'

'You reckon? I've got the nick written all over me. Well I'm going to use it. Those people, those do-gooders, will believe anything. The worse the better. And Madam can't deny it, she's not allowed to. I can't wait to get out.' She got up. 'Sorry Miss Clarke, but I don't need your help.'

'Dismissed,' thought Miss Clarke as Lily walked across to Sandra. Not unduly depressed by her lack of success (for she was used to it), she went on to her next case, in South Wing.

Meanwhile, Lily had found Sandra, who had come out of her cell. They sat chatting together.

'How're you this morning, luv?'

'OK,' said Sandra in a voice of utmost depression.

'Still missing your baby?' Lily's voice was deeply sympathetic. Sandra nodded. 'Mustn't let it get you down. Try and look forward to when you see 'im again. If he don't get ill or nothing, that is.'

This was cold comfort and Sandra looked more depressed than ever. She was almost crying. Lily felt delighted. Get 'em right down and then they did what you wanted.

'You see Sandra,' she added, 'the nick's okay if you know your way about. But you've got to learn it. Need someone like me to fill you in.'

Sandra nodded. 'You're kind,' she said.

Lily looked up and saw Mrs Armitage was coming through the gates. 'Blast her, she would,' thought Lily.

The Chief came up to her. 'Why aren't you working?' she asked. 'Stand up!'

Lily did so with a bad grace and Sandra, too, stood up.

'Well?'

Lily searched for an excuse and found one.

'I'm not at work miss, because I'm waiting to be seen by the Welfare Officer,' she said, lying in her teeth.

'Right,' said the Chief. 'Wait outside your own cell where she won't miss you.'

Lily, with a superior smile on her lips, mooched across to the bench outside her cell, dragging her feet as she went. Sandra stood twisting her hands together, looking at the ground. She was terrified of Mrs Armitage.

'And you,' the Chief was saying. 'Sandra isn't it?'

'Yes miss.'

'Why aren't you working?'

'I haven't been given no work Miss.'

'Why not?'

'I don't know Miss,' Sandra's voice was hardly more than a whisper.

The Chief saw Pat Berryman coming out of Janet Harker's office and strode across to her. She looked furious and even the officer felt alarmed.

'Why hasn't that girl Sandra been assigned some work?' demanded Mrs Armitage.

'She's still very upset, Chief.'

And indeed Sandra was now crying, as quietly as possible. Whether because of her baby, or from sheer terror of Mrs Armitage, will never be known.

'The doctor passed her fit.'

'I know.' Pat Berryman started to argue. 'But Miss Harker said to give her time to recover.'

'She'll recover a lot quicker if she's not sitting around here, moping. So get her on to a working party quick. And Lily Hever too.'

'Yes Chief,' said the officer. And then unwisely added, 'Vivien Pearce was saying that it might be a good thing if Sandra did a Domestic Science course.'

'So Vivien Pearce is running the Wing now? When I want her advice I'll ask for it.'

The Chief went out slamming the gate aggressively, locking it behind her.

Pat Berryman sighed. Sometimes the Chief Officer made her feel just as though she was an inmate herself.

'Come along, Sandra,' she said and glanced round for Lily Hever. But Lily had heard what the Chief had said and had made herself scarce. She had no intention of working until she had to. Besides the doctor hadn't seen her yet. After all those months shut up alone she wasn't fit. Lily had conveniently forgotten that she had been shut up entirely at her own request.

* * *

A week or two later, Lily and Sandra were sitting on the bench outside Sandra's cell discussing, as usual, Sandra's baby.

'I only hope they treat him right,' said Lily, deliberately making herself sound worried.

'Who?'

'The foster parents.'

'Miss Clarke said. . . .'

'Her!' Lily's voice was full of scorn. 'Everybody knows them foster homes are only in it for the money.'

'Oh, no!' Sandra sounded horrified.

'They don't care what the kids eat or wear. If you don't give 'em a bit extra, they keep 'em half starved.'

'I didn't know that,' Sandra sounded worried. 'Nobody told me.'

'No skin off their nose.'

'What can I do?'

Lily shrugged. 'Nothing, if you haven't the money.'

'I have got some saved. Just a bit. I saved it for the baby.'

'How much?'

'About seventy-five quid.'

There was a pause, while Lily digested this welcome piece of news. Then she said:

'Tell you what. I'm going out before you. If you'd trust me, I could collect it, make sure they got a couple of pounds a week, say. I could make sure he was properly looked after.'

Sandra, who was a very stupid girl, turned eagerly to Lily.

'Would you, Lily, would you really?'

Lily patted her knee.

'For a pal? Course I would.'

Fran had been listening to this conversation, only catching a word here and there, but enough for her to realise that Lily was up to her tricks again. She didn't intend to get involved, but someone ought to know.

It was growing near to dinner time and the other inmates

were drifting back into the Wing. Vivien, who had been in the library, came up a little later than everybody else.

As she did so, Fran signalled to her, secretly, as though she didn't want anyone else to know. Vivien went and sat next to her.

'What is it?'

'It's her, that bitch,' and Fran nodded to where Lily and Sandra sat. 'The kid's your cell mate, isn't she?'

'Yes.'

'Well, you better do something about it. Stop that Tiger Lily getting her claws into her.'

'It's difficult. They're on the same working party. Anyhow what could she do to Sandra?'

Fran's dark eyes flashed. 'Don't you know about her? Never been in before, have you? That one, she's poison. She'll find out things and use them against you. She blackmailed a mate of mine once, then grassed on 'er.'

'But Sandra doesn't have anything worth taking.'

'That don't matter.' Fran's voice was urgent. 'She likes getting her hooks into someone, and then watching 'em squirm. Keep an eye on 'em and break it up.'

'Why don't you break it up?' Vivien did not take this as seriously as Fran did.

'I daren't. Don't trust meself.'

Vivien remembered some story she had heard about Fran and Lily.

'OK. I'll do what I can. Now let's go and get our dinners.'

Janet Harker was standing at the door of her office. Miss Berryman was by her side. There was a frown on her usually smiling face:

'What is it?' asked Janet.

'I don't know. But I smell trouble.'

'What sort of trouble?'

'There's tension. I can feel it building up.'

'I can't say I've noticed anything,' said Janet, who thought Berryman sometimes talked too much.

Just then, Mrs Armitage came onto the Wing like a tornado. She was obviously in a very bad temper.

'Excuse me, Miss Harker, but could I have a word with Miss Berryman?'

'Of course,' said Janet, thinking with amusement that the Chief observed protocol to an unnecessary degree. Mrs Armitage turned to Pat Berryman.

'Why did you put Sandra Logan and that Hever woman on the same working party?' she asked accusingly.

For a moment Pat was thrown, then she answered. 'It was you who told me to get them working, Chief.'

'Yes, but not together!' said Mrs Armitage most unfairly, for when she gave her her orders she had not stipulated anything of the sort.

'Anyone with any nose could have seen the result of that "friendship",' continued Mrs Armitage. 'It's bad enough that it was allowed to start in the first place.'

Janet Harker was beginning to get angry. 'Are you criticising the way I run my Wing, Mrs Armitage?'

'No Miss Harker. But there's something brewing up here, and I don't like the smell of it.'

At one end of the table Lily and Sandra had finished their meal. Sandra, who did not smoke but who had been induced by Lily to buy cigarettes (for this was a levy which Lily always exacted from her victims), offered one to her friend who took it, lit it, and blew luxuriantly through her nose. Sandra had, in her slow way, been thinking, as she had her lunch.

'About that money,' she said.

'Yeah?'

'I mean, how do I know you'll give it to the foster people?'

Lily restrained a strong desire to hit the girl; instead she said sweetly:

'I'm your mate, ain't I?'

'Yeah. But it's a lot of money.'

'A lousy seventy-five quid? That's chicken feed compared to what I got waiting for me.' She looked at Sandra and smiled sadly. 'I was going to add a bit to it, on me own, without telling you, like. But if you don't even trust me—'

Sandra was instantly upset.

'Forget it. It's your kid. If you don't care what happens to him—'

She got up and sauntered towards the bench where they usually sat, and Sandra, after a moment, followed her.

After some further talk, Sandra was completely subdued and eating out of Lily's hand. The older woman felt delighted with her work. She had found out where Sandra's savings were, and had arranged for the girl to give her an authority to collect them. This she would then smuggle out of the prison when she left. Seventy-five pounds! It would make the whole difference. Mentally Lily was budgeting. A decent set of clothes, a night at a London hotel, a hairdo and a manicure, and she would be ready to start her life of fraud again. Fortunately she had a smart suitcase. Eastbourne would be nice, she thought; she'd never been there. She was so deep in her day dream that she hardly noticed when Vivien appeared and said:

'Hullo Sandra. Here's someone who wants to meet you.'

The someone was Cecily Foyle who had come to arrange with Vivien about her pre-release home visit in two days time.

'Feeling excited?' she had asked Vivien, who had answered that she was indeed. She had then suggested that Mrs Foyle should talk to Sandra with a view to visiting her. Perhaps she could woo Sandra away from Lily? In any case prison life was becoming daily less real to Vivien and less important. Soon she would be out and free and able to live again.

Cecily Foyle had followed Vivien up to the bench. 'Hullo Sandra,' she said, 'I'm Cecily Foyle. I'm Vivien's visitor. When she goes, would you like me to come and see you?'

There was a pause. Sandra looked blank.

Lily Hever did not budge but sat listening to every word.

'Are you from the Welfare?' asked Sandra.

'No. I'm just a friendly face, I suppose. Someone you can talk things over with.'

'Yeah,' said Sandra.

Hardly an inspiring conversation, thought Cecily. Still, she persevered.

'Maybe we can have a proper chat next time I come round. I'd like that.'

Lily felt it was time to drop a little venom into the conversation.

'Oh sure,' she said. 'You'd like that, Mrs Foyle. You'd get a kick out of it.'

Cecily was so taken aback that she didn't answer immediately, then:

'What do you mean?' she asked.

'Come off it. You wouldn't give us the time of day if you met us outside. It's like visiting the monkeys at the Zoo, inn'it?'

'On the contrary,' said Cecily.

'You've nothing to say to us and you bloody well know it. And you only listen because you're paid to.'

Cecily refused to lose her temper. 'In the first place,' she said, 'I am not paid to come here. In the second place I don't think you are on my list. I was talking to Sandra.'

'Well, she don't want to talk to you. Do you love?'

Sandra was silent, confused, unable to look at Cecily. She didn't answer.

'See?' said Lily triumphantly. 'So you can shove off.'

Cecily left, almost in tears from sheer anger. On the Centre she ran into Martha Parrish and Miss Clarke who both asked her what was the matter.

'It's Lily Hever. She really is the most offensive person I've ever met.'

'She can be very difficult,' agreed Miss Clarke.

'Difficult!' said Cecily. 'I nearly punched her on the nose.'

'Yes,' said Martha Parrish seriously. 'She does have that effect on people.'

'Have you fixed things up with Vivien?' asked the Welfare Officer, to change the subject.

'Yes, it's all arranged. I'm driving her to Salisbury, and her father's meeting us there. Then I shall go to my friends, who live nearby, for the weekend and pick Vivien up on Sunday. Her family have asked me to supper. I think she's wild with excitement at getting out.'

That night Sandra wept again for the first time in several nights. She was as usual somewhat incoherent.

'It's my baby,' she said. 'Those people he's with. They don't take care. They're only in it for the money.'

'Who told you?' asked Vivien.

'Lily.'

'I bet she did,' thought Vivien, and resolved to have a word with Miss Harker the next day. In the event something happened which drove everything except her own concerns completely out of her head.

Each landing of each Wing came separately to the Library to change their books in parties of twenty or thirty prisoners. The following afternoon Miss Dudgeon brought a party from North Wing, with, among others, Fran Morris and an extremely handsome woman who was in for a very short sentence. She was smartly dressed and looked, thought Vivien, who was beginning to adopt the vivid language of the other inmates, like a high class scrubber. The woman glanced at Vivien and smiled to herself, and then turned away and looked at the books on the shelves.

Vivien had by now learnt that by far the most popular books were thrillers and romances. A few of the inmates who were studying for exams took out specialist books. One inmate, a rather crazy Welshwoman, invariably took out the Bible which she read avidly, alone in her cell.

Fran came up, a copy of an Ed McBain novel in her hand. 'That was lovely,' she said, 'all them murders. And that bit on the roof. I'll go and choose another. I've brought old Lizzie's book back; Harker said I could; the old girl isn't feeling too good today.'

And she laid a children's book with big coloured pictures on the desk.

'Why don't you take one of the women's magazines for Lizzie? *Woman* is doing a feature on Princess Anne this week.'

'Good idea. I'll do that,' said Fran and went across to choose herself a book with plenty of bloodshed in it.

For half an hour Vivien was busy. Miss Dudgeon, who had been having a good gossip with the officer in charge, looked at her watch and called out; and the women, talking and arguing, started to move towards the door which was, of course, locked.

Vivien looked up. The well dressed prostitute stood in front of her. She was holding her book, which was a copy of *Valley of the Dolls*. 'Brought this back,' she said in a low husky voice.

'Thanks. What are you taking out?'

'Nothing. Getting out of this hole tomorrow. Thanks luv. Good luck.' She looked at Vivien as though something amused her, and joined the group at the door, which Miss Dudgeon had now unlocked.

Vivien picked up the book to stamp it as returned. She saw that it had a paper between the leaves. She called to the woman whose name she could not remember.

'There's a paper here. D'you want it?'

But the woman had joined the rest of the prisoners and had gone through the door.

It was very quiet in the library now the inmates had gone. Vivien picked the paper out of the book. She might as well read it, she thought.

CHAPTER EIGHT

The next morning Faye was talking to her Deputy when Penny appeared at the door.

'Mrs Foyle is here,' she said. 'Could you see her madam?'

Cecily came in.

'Sorry to bother you,' she said. 'But something rather odd has happened. Vivien Pearce absolutely refuses to go with me for her home visit today.

'Refuses?' said two surprised voices. And Radley added. 'No one ever turns down a chance to get out of here.'

'Did you speak to her?' asked Faye.

'Of course. She apologised for wasting my time, but she flatly refuses to go. And two days ago she was so keen.'

'I wonder if Janet Harker noticed anything,' said Faye.

'It's her day off,' said Radley. 'I'll go and have a word with Vivien. There must be something behind it. She's such a sensible girl.'

'You do that Charles. And report back to me later. I've got to go through the mail with Mr Morton.'

'There's just one thing,' said Cecily. 'She looks quite ill this morning, not at all like herself, with great lines under her eyes.'

When Radley next saw Faye, he could only report that he too had had no luck with Vivien.

'She's not irrational about it. Just determined.'

'I can't understand it,' said Faye. 'I'll have to talk to her myself. It's all the fault of that man.'

'Max Stern?'

'Yes.'

'What d'you mean?' Radley sounded impatient. 'Stern is

inside doing ten years. The girl was keen to go out yesterday, and today refuses to. Do you suggest that. . . .'

Faye interrupted. 'No Charles. I don't suggest anything. I was thinking of Vivien. If it hadn't been for him she would never have been here. Imagine what it must feel like to have wasted nearly two years of her life, for that man?'

She rang Penny. 'I want Vivien Pearce sent up,' she said, and added to Radley. 'I'll see her in here, she's more likely to talk. Will you stay?'

'Better not. I was totally unsuccessful with her just now. You'd do better alone.' And as he left he added. 'Liz Clarke is on the war path.'

'What now?'

'Mrs Foyle told her that the girl Sandra is having morbid fears about the baby being ill-treated in that home, which she took as a direct affront to her arrangements.'

Faye sighed. Sometimes she felt the staff's clashing personalities were more than she could cope with. Aloud she said. 'Sandra should never have left K block. Peter slipped up there I think.'

Penny put her head round the door to say that Vivien had arrived.

'Bring her in,' said Faye, 'as soon as Mr Radley has left.'

Vivien was as usual extremely polite. She sat with her hands folded, avoiding Faye's glance. In some indefinable way she had changed; the spring had gone out of her step and her smile was mechanical.

'I'm sorry madam,' she was saying, 'but I don't want to go on my home visit.'

'You have had a letter from your parents which has upset you?'

'No madam. . . .'

'It is nothing to do with Max Stern?'

There was an infinitesimal pause, but the girl's voice was quite level as she answered, 'No madam.'

'Sometimes I feel you still worry about him.'

Vivien smiled at this, but it was a warped, bitter smile. She didn't answer.

'You're still young. One error of judgment shouldn't be allowed to ruin your whole life.'

'No madam.'

'I'm getting nowhere with the girl,' thought Faye, but she persevered.

'It's none of my business, but do you really care so much for him?'

A pause and then Vivien spoke vehemently. 'No. I do not.' And she added quickly. 'None of this has anything to do with Max, madam.'

'Then why don't you want to go out and start a new life?'

There was another pause before Vivien said: 'There's nothing for me outside madam.' It seemed to Faye that she was in torment despite her quiet words.

'You know that your job is waiting for you. I had a letter from one of the Directors. They want you back.'

'It's kind of them. But I'm not going back there. I'm not going anywhere where anyone knows me.'

She spoke almost as though she was afraid. Did she think that people were going to condemn her? Faye suddenly realised why this girl was so sympathetic to her. She was the same age her own daughter would have been had she lived. Vivien had the same sort of looks, too, as Virginia would have had. Faye got up and went over to sit next to Vivien.

'I'm not trying to pry. I just want to understand. You have coped so magnificently in here; we all admired you for it; and now you seem to have changed. What is it? Can I do anything to help?'

It was no longer a governor talking to a prisoner. Vivien sensed this and decided to take advantage of it.

'There is one thing. Could I have my cell to myself again? The Wing isn't so full this week. Perhaps Miss Harker could arrange something for Sandra. I think I shall go mad if. . . .' She broke off. One had to be careful what one said to these people. With a shock she realised that the emphasis had shifted. The staff and the governor had become 'them', and there was now an impenetrable gulf between them and Vivien. She had begun to think as a prisoner thinks.

Faye, quite unaware of her thoughts, answered kindly. 'Yes I think I could arrange that. I gather that Sandra is worried over her baby.'

'You can say that again,' said Vivien ironically.

'But about your problem. Would you like to have a chat with Miss Clarke or one of the psychiatrists? They might be able to help you.'

Vivien's voice rose. 'Oh for God's sake leave me alone.'

She apologised instantly, but Faye realised the interview was at an end and sent her back to the Wing.

Faye sat, depressed. Total failure. Ah well, Vivien would be out in three weeks now, and then it was up to Miss Clarke to make arrangements for her. Meanwhile she rang through to Miss Harker and told her to move Sandra out of Vivien's cell, if she could manage this.

Vivien went straight back to the library and apologised to Mrs Spencer, the officer on duty, for being late, explaining that she had been sent for by madam.

'To discuss your home visit I suppose,' said Mrs Spencer happily, and added, 'You might go through the thriller section. All the books want tidying; they do manage to leave them in such a mess. And bring me any that need rebinding.'

It was late when Vivien returned to the Wing. She was even later than she need have been because she had made a detour and gone to the Hospital Wing where she knew she would find Sister, if not Dr Mayes himself. She was lucky, for he was alone in his surgery, about to go off duty.

'Hullo,' he said. 'Are you a messenger of doom?' and grinned at Vivien whom he liked. She summoned up her most charming smile.

'No message Doctor,' she said. 'I'm taking advantage of this,' and she tapped the red band she wore. 'I've no business to ask you, but I wondered if you'd give me a sleeping pill. I had a rotten night.'

'You could have waited till the morning.'

'It's tonight I want to sleep.'

'Anything wrong?'

Peter Mayes was in a hurry to get away and did not notice her drawn face and shadowed eyes.

'No.'

He went to the medicine cupboard and gave her a pill.

'Worrying about getting out? It does take people like that. You've no business to come asking me; don't do it again.' But he smiled as he said it, which took the sting out of his words. As she went away, after thanking him, he called out: 'Have a good home visit.'

If only more of our customers were like this girl, he thought: and put on his coat and went to meet a colleague at his old hospital.

Supper was in progress when Vivien returned to the Wing. She took a tray and went to her cell. To her surprise Sandra's belongings had already been moved. The Governor certainly moved fast, thought Vivien. I wish I hadn't snapped at her like that. She is a nice woman and she was really trying to help.

On the Wing curious eyes regarded her cell: for already everybody knew that she had refused to go on her home visit.

Sandra had been put in a cell with Reba. This didn't please either of them, for Reba, like many people who professed deep religious convictions, found it very hard to be sympathetic with the troubles of ordinary human beings. She had no desire to hear Sandra's moans over her wretched baby.

At the moment, Sandra was as usual sitting with Lily, who was in a very foul temper. 'If they had to move the kid, why couldn't they have moved her in with me?'

She proceeded to take it out on Sandra who was shortly in tears. Across the Wing Fran watched them. She wondered for how much longer she would be able to keep her temper with Lily. She'd seen her at work before, twice with tragic results. That snooty girl Vivien had proved to be no help, she thought. And what Madam and the Chief had been up to letting Lily out she couldn't imagine. Though come to think of it, the Chief hadn't seemed at all pleased about it. A woman hurrying past trod on her foot. Fran turned and cursed her. Lily, who was nearer to Fran than she cared for, hastily moved away in the direction of the office, and in doing so collided with Pat Berryman.

'Careful Lily,' she said.

'Sorry miss.' Lily was using her meek voice. 'But it's that Fran. She isn't safe she isn't. She scares the living daylights out of me.'

Cringing, she scuttled away to her cell.

Fran had always been a planner. A year or two before she had thought out a wily scheme during some alterations to the prison. The work was done by men from Cricklewood Prison, and Fran had managed to plan a scheme whereby a friend of hers on the Wing had been able to be alone for a while each day with her husband who was part of the working party. Lily had found out about this and had of course given their plan away. Fran had never forgiven her. Now she was planning a way in which to pay Lily back. She was whispering to her friends, outlining her plan. Janet Harker was perfectly aware something was up, but Fran's schemes were usually harmless (except for the time when, inspired by a Colditz story, Fran had nearly brought off another prisoners' escape); besides the excitement was good for the prisoners and prevented that deadly feeling of monotony and boredom which pervades most prisons.

But now, there was no doubt about it, thought Pat Berryman, tension was mounting in the Wing. She didn't like it and was thankful when Mrs Armitage appeared.

'Everything all right?'

'Not really,' said Pat. 'There's something funny in the atmosphere. Nothing's happened, but. . . .'

'I'll stay late tonight, till lock up,' said the Chief, and added. 'You know, Miss Berryman, you've the makings of a good prison officer in you, some day.'

The next morning, at breakfast, a tray was spilt as Fran with her loaded tray cannoned sharply into Reba who was also carrying one. Plates, cutlery and food went crashing to the floor. Some of the inmates cursed, some laughed, and old Lizzie came to the door of her cell to see what the row was about.

'Look where you're going Fran,' called Pat Berryman.

Fran seemed flustered.

'Sorry miss,' she muttered.

'Come on. Get this cleaned up. Get a pail and a brush Reba, and Fran you pick up the things on the floor.'

Fran stooped, pleased that her plan had worked. As she picked up the cutlery and cleared up the mess, she managed to slip a knife up her sleeve. She moved fast, and by the time Reba had arrived with a broom and pail, both trays with the debris and cutlery had gone out to the trolley where the dirty things were kept.

That evening at supper Lily beckoned Sandra across. She hadn't seen her much during the day.

'How did you get on last night luv?' she asked.

Sandra seemed far more lively than usual.

'Reba? I didn't like it Lily. She prays a lot out loud. Wish I could have stayed with Vivien.'

Lily was thoughtful. Why hadn't Vivien gone on her home visit? Something was up. Sandra was still talking. Better listen in case it was anything that affected her, thought Lily.

'Still, it won't be long now.'

'What won't?' asked Lily.

'I saw Miss Clarke today. Guess what? I can have my baby back for the rest of my sentence. She said Madam always thought it was a mistake him going. She was right at that. Isn't it wonderful Lily?'

For a moment Lily was too taken aback to speak. She saw her seventy-five pounds disappear and with it the chance of her new life. Sandra was still chattering on. Silly little bugger. Blind rage took hold of Lily and she seized Sandra's arm and twisted it.

Across the Wing Fran was watching.

Suddenly Sandra screamed a high thin scream, then got up and ran into her cell.

Lily looked up. Fran stood in front of her, and she was holding a knife. Several of the other women were behind Fran. They were party to her carefully laid plan, to frighten the daylights out of Lily. The whole thing was only a feint.

But to Lily it was no feint. She backed away towards her cell, but she was surrounded on all sides now. She looked wildly round. Hadn't Madam promised protection? But there were no screws in evidence for the moment. Dudgeon was busy having a good laugh with old Lizzie. Janet Harker and Berryman were in the office. Suddenly events started to move very fast.

'Going somewhere?' asked Fran, quietly.

Lily started to whimper. Fran's voice was almost a whisper.

'I've waited over a year to get even with you, Lily Hever. Now I'm going to carve you up. Teach you a lesson you won't forget.'

Vivien appeared at the door of her cell. The women had closed in on Lily; and Fran had got her by the shoulder. All this in utter silence. 'It's horrible,' thought Vivien. 'Better if the women screamed and cursed.'

And then, as they swayed towards her, she was there too among the struggling group, surrounding Lily who was trying to escape to her cell.

Miss Harker, struck by the unusual silence of the Wing, came to her door. She saw at once what was happening and blew on her whistle.

'Stop it!' she called. 'Break it up.'

She was quickly joined by the two prison officers, who joined the struggling women. Suddenly Lily Hever screamed, a piercing scream. The women stopped, frozen in their tracks. Lily had fallen to her knees, moaning and trying to clutch at the knife which was sticking out of the lower part of her back. She gasped and fell on her face.

Fran was transfixed with horror.

'I didn't mean,' she was muttering. 'I didn't mean. . . .'

Miss Harker was on her knees by Lily.

'She's alive,' she said.

Pat Berryman came out of the office. 'I rang the doctor,' she said.

Still the women stood transfixed, staring. They were none of them murderers, merely petty criminals, prostitutes, drunks. They had been playing a game with a woman they all hated, and now the game had gone wrong.

'Into your cells!' said Berryman and into their cells they went like zombies. Vivien was already in hers, trembling all over.

Soon the women had all been locked in, to the extreme bewilderment of old Lizzie who had been having one of her deaf days and had missed the whole episode.

Fran was sitting on the edge of her bed rocking herself to and fro, her big body shaken by sobs. How had it happened?

She hadn't knifed Lily, she was sure she hadn't. But who was going to believe that?

In her cell Vivien was standing staring at what little sky showed through the square window. She was still trembling. Suddenly she went to the pail and was violently and horribly sick.

Faye was just leaving when the telephone in her office rang. It was Janet Harker. Faye listened, then: 'Thank you,' she said. 'I'll come at once.'

She replaced the receiver and stood for a moment. It seemed that Lily was not too badly hurt; she was conscious when moved to the Hospital Wing.

'Thank God for that,' thought Faye. For she knew that if Lily Hever died, she would have murdered her.

CHAPTER NINE

Faye went straight to the Hospital Wing. But Dr Mayes had no time to speak to her.

She stood near the door of the emergency room where Lily lay, hoping someone would give her news. Sister, a rubber apron over her starched one, came out, gave her a brief nod and vanished. A nurse came out carrying a blood-stained bundle of clothing. Faye recognised Lily's shabby old prison uniform which she had insisted on wearing. A young doctor carrying a covered kidney bowl came out, and Sister returned carrying a bottle of blood. No-one noticed Faye, she might have been a shadow on the wall. She heard an occasional word from the two doctors.

'Better try her blood pressure again . . . in shock all right . . . we'll need more blood. . . . Ah, thank you Sister. Now. . . .'

Then Mayes' voice. 'Doubt if she'll. . . .'

Through the open door Faye caught a glimpse of Lily's unconscious face, colourless and very still. Then the door swung shut and Faye was alone, while the medical staff fought for the life of a woman who had been nothing but a nuisance and whom no-one had liked, but whose life must be saved if it were humanly possible.

Faye went to the wards which had been left in charge of a young and rather frightened probationer.

'I am going to North Wing,' she said, 'if Dr Mayes asks for me.'

'Yes Madam.'

The Governor wondered if Mrs Armitage was on North Wing and prayed that she was not. She did not know how she would meet her Chief's eyes. . . .

It was strangely quiet on the Wing, usually one of the noisiest places in the prison. The inmates sat or stood: waiting, it seemed for news. In her cell Fran was rocking herself to and fro muttering over and over again, 'I only did it to frighten her.'

In her cell, Vivien was standing, her head resting on the upper bunk. She looked up at Faye but didn't speak. The Governor smiled at her but she did not react in any way, only stood frozen. 'Why?' thought Faye. 'Why is she so upset? I didn't know she had any dealings with Lily at all.'

Faye moved on towards the Assistant Governor's office, where Janet Harker was waiting for her.

'Any news Madam?' she asked.

'She's very ill. They're doing all they can. I left a message for Dr Mayes to ring through.'

'Yes Madam.'

Everybody seemed strangely formal, Faye thought. And nobody would meet her eyes. Then the gate was unlocked and the Deputy and Mrs Armitage came through.

The Chief took in the situation at a glance. 'M'm,' she thought. 'More like Martha Parrish's Wing.' (For the Assistant Governor of South Wing was proud that hers was known as the Quiet Wing, although the noisier inmates knew it as The Graveyard.)

Radley turned to Janet Harker. 'Could we borrow your office for a moment?' he asked.

'Of course,' said Janet.

'Thanks,' said Radley and the Governor went in, followed by the Chief and Radley himself. Radley shut the door. 'The Chief has something to say,' he said.

Faye noticed that Mrs Armitage had more colour than usual in her face and seemed for a moment tongue tied. When she spoke, the words came out in a rush.

'It's about Hever,' she said. 'I know you went against us all in bringing her back on the Wing, and maybe now you're wishing you hadn't. Well Madam, maybe you were right and maybe you were wrong: but we all know that you thought you were doing it for the best, and so' (a pause) 'we'll all stand by you.'

Faye was immeasurably moved by this proof of loyalty from this strong obstinate woman. She would have liked to have taken her hands and thanked her, even kissed her, but, knowing how much she would have hated it, she only said: 'Thank you Chief. Thank you very much. All of you.'

The telephone on Janet's desk rang. Radley answered it. He listened. Then he said: 'I'll tell her,' and turning to Faye, 'Lily died five minutes ago.'

There was a pause before Faye said. 'I'll go.' Then she turned to her Deputy.

'This will have to be treated as murder. Charles, will you ring the police?'

Even in death, Lily looked disagreeable, though rather handsome. Faye and Peter Mayes looked down at her for a moment.

'Poor woman,' she said.

The doctor drew the sheet over the dead woman's face and took Faye's arm as they walked towards the Centre.

'She hadn't a chance,' he said. 'When she first came in I thought she wasn't too badly injured, just a superficial stab wound. But when I examined her I found that the point of the knife had ruptured her spleen. She started a massive haemorrhage almost at once.' Faye was silent for a moment. 'We'll have to explain it to the police. Charles has rung them, they'll be here any moment.'

As she spoke they heard the siren as the police cars stopped outside the prison.

'I hope it won't be that fellow Laurence,' said the doctor. 'I don't care for him, he's a bossy sort of man.'

Faye agreed, though she did not say so: all she said was, 'I'd better go to my office to be ready for him.' And added, 'do you think we've time for a quick drink?'

Unfortunately it *was* Chief Inspector Laurence, accompanied by a sharply dressed young sergeant, and a posse of photographers, finger print men, forensic officers and other minions. He was taken up to North Wing where he gave his instructions to his henchmen, and then down to the Governor's room where Faye and some of her colleagues were interviewed by him.

It was not a particularly amicable interview, as the Inspector was very annoyed that Lily's body had been moved. He did not seem to understand that Lily had been taken to hospital, while still conscious. When the doctor had convinced him of this, he turned to the matter of the knife.

'It was one of your canteen knives you say?'

'Yes.'

'I suppose several people have handled it. It's going to be difficult to find conclusive finger prints.'

There was an edge on the Doctor's voice as he answered. 'Oddly enough, we were trying to save the wretched woman's life when we took it out.'

Faye felt it was time to intervene. 'You have our full co-operation, Inspector. Just say what you want.'

'Thank you, Mrs Boswell. All I want is for everything to be left to the Police. I don't want the women to have any doubt about who is in charge.'

Faye could gladly have hit him. Instead she said quietly. 'Very well.'

After some further talk concerning the inmates, the Inspector asked to go to North Wing, adding, 'I must ask specifically for all the questioning to be left to me.'

Faye and Charles Radley looked at each other.

On North Wing the Inspector's minions had been busy. He had earlier been up with them and had left his technicians behind. Acting on his instructions they had made a chalk mark showing where Lily had lain, and had photographed the scene. The women, subdued and rather frightened, stood at the doors of their cells.

The Inspector took up his stance near the door of the office. Mrs Armitage stood nearby.

'Now . . . ladies . . .' he said. 'You were all here when the stabbing took place. I'd like you to stand exactly, or as close as you remember, to where you were when it happened.'

None of the women budged an inch.

'Come on,' said the Inspector, raising his voice.

Again no-one moved. Radley nodded to Mrs Armitage, who raised her voice.

'Come along,' she said. 'You heard!'

Slowly the women moved to their original places and went through the motions of miming the stabbing.

'Who was holding the knife?' asked the Inspector.

There was a pause. No-one answered, and then one of the women nudged Mrs Armitage and whispered something to her.

'What's that?' asked the Inspector.

'She says it was this woman,' said the Chief and pointed to Fran Morris.

'Is this true?' the Inspector asked Fran. There was a pause, then suddenly a chorus of voices answered him.

'Yes, it was her got the knife to put the frighteners on Lily,' and Reba added, 'she got the shiv when the trays upset at breakfast.'

Fran stood, hugging herself. She was looking very frightened.

'Thank you,' said the Inspector. 'If the women could go to their cells, Mrs Armitage; and then my sergeant will take individual statements, if one of your officers would accompany him. And I would like to interview this woman, Fran Morris. Perhaps I could borrow your office, Mr Radley? And if you and Mrs Boswell would come too?'

In Radley's office the Inspector seated himself behind the desk with Faye, Radley and the Chief ranged behind him. Fran was brought in by two prison officers who stood stiffly on each side of her. As Faye watched, the whole thing had an unreality about it as though she was watching a play. There was a great bitterness in her heart. If she had let Lily have her own way, she would have still been locked up in her cell and Fran would have been on the verge of completing her sentence. As it was, she would certainly be charged, and later would go to court to be awarded a much longer sentence.

The Inspector was asking Fran all the usual questions; her age, name, prison number, crime, length of sentence: now he had asked her some personal questions which had evidently annoyed her, for her quick temper flared up as she answered: 'Get lost!'

'That attitude won't help you,' said the Inspector.

'I don't need no help.'

'I think you do. We know the knife was yours.'

'Who says?' demanded Fran.

'And we know you organised the disturbance so that you could get at Lily Hever. It's no good denying it.'

Fran glanced at him. 'I'm not saying nothing,' she said.

'We know too that she was terrified of you and that you had it in for her.'

'She was a grass. A lousy stinking grass.'

'Exactly. So you wanted her out of the way.'

'But I didn't kill her.' Fran's voice was growing desperate.

'You set the whole thing up,' said the Inspector.

'Only to frighten 'er.'

'So you admit it.'

'I don't admit nothing. OK, OK, I stole the shiv. But only to frighten 'er. She got 'er hooks into somebody, see? A kid called Sandra. I just wanted to warn 'er off.'

'But in the heat of the struggle, you lost your head and stabbed her.'

Fran was beginning to panic. 'No! That's not how it was. I only wanted to warn her off Sandra and scare her at the same time. I owed her an old score. God's my witness, I didn't want to do more than scare her and then, in the struggle, someone snatched the knife out of my hand.'

'Come off it,' said the Inspector inelegantly.

'It's true, I swear it's true. I'm a bit of a nutter, but I'd never kill Lily: she wasn't worth it.' Fran was incoherent. 'And now I'll lose my remission and be here for years more.'

At the words 'I'll lose my remission,' something seemed to click in Faye's brain. What a fool she had been! She went up to the Inspector and spoke to him, quietly. When she had finished: 'Very well,' he said, 'I am sure you would not ask this unless you had good reason, Mrs Boswell. Mrs Armitage, will you take this woman to her cell. See she is locked in, and bring her back in, say an hour.'

'Thank you, Inspector,' said Faye as Fran, bewildered now, was removed by the prison officers. 'And I will have some tea and sandwiches sent up for you and the sergeant.'

Faye paused at the entrance to Vivien's cell. Vivien was pacing up and down restlessly.

The Wing was still quieter than usual, but seemed to be getting back to normal.

Faye glanced at her watch. It was not yet seven o'clock, only three hours since all this had started.

Vivien looked up and saw the Governor standing in her door. She stopped pacing.

'Now Vivien. Sit down.' Faye sat at the table opposite the

girl. 'I thought I should tell you that the Inspector is going to accuse Fran of Lily's murder.'

Vivien looked up and stared at Faye.

'What does Fran say?'

'She denies it of course. She says that it was all a put up job to frighten Lily and that the knife was snatched out of her hand. The Inspector doesn't believe her.'

Vivien looked down. She couldn't meet Faye's eyes any more.

'I did it,' she said. Her voice was practically inaudible.

'I thought you might have. . . . But *why* Vivien? Why?'

'Lily was nothing to me. I never meant to kill her. Only to wound her. I was going to own up at once. And then the news came that she was dying. And then. . . .' She shrugged hopelessly.

'You haven't answered my question. *Why*?'

'So that I'd lose my remission and get an extra sentence. It was the only chance I had.'

'Chance of what?'

'To stay alive. You see, there was this girl who returned her book the day before yesterday and there was this paper in it and. . . .' She got up and went to her locker and took out a piece of paper which she laid in front of Faye.

> *'So you shopped me my little Viv did you?*
> *I have friends. They'll be waiting when*
> *you come out. Remember Annie. Max.'*

Faye read it with cold horror.

'Who is this Annie?'

'A girl with a terribly scarred face. She was the one who put the law on to my flat. Soon after I came in here I saw in the paper that she had disappeared, and later she was found dead.'

'And he threatened to do the same to you?'

Vivien nodded.

'You didn't shop him over the heroin, did you?'

'I didn't even know he dealt in it. But what's the use? Once I'm outside they'll get me. My only hope is to stay in here.'

Faye looked at her. She was stooped, like a much older woman. Her voice was flat. Faye remembered her as she was before, and felt murderous towards Max Stern.

'Vivien,' she said. 'You must tell the police what you've just told me.'

'The police!' There was infinite scorn in Vivien's voice.

'They could stop these people, trace them and . . .'

Vivien interrupted her. 'It's no good. I daren't go out as long as Max is alive. I never meant to kill Lily, but if I swear in Court it was deliberate maybe they'll give me a really long stretch. Then I'll be safe.' And she added. 'Poor Lily. She was a bitch but she did me a good turn.'

Before Vivien was taken to the police station to be charged, Faye had a word with the Inspector, who was not very encouraging.

'Once a girl's out, if Max Stern wants to get her, there's nothing and no-one could stop him,' he said positively. 'He's got friends outside and they'll do what he says.'

When Vivien's case came into court, she put up such a show of aggression and insolence that she got, as she wished, a long sentence and was transferred to the Long Term Wing. As time went on she would no doubt become an embittered woman, unpopular with both officers and prisoners. Faye could hardly bear to consider it, for she had been such very promising material.

Fran lost some remission, but not a great deal, and was then released, while Sandra had already been persuaded that the best thing for her to do was to have her baby back and return to Maternity, which she did the following week.

And Lily Hever? She was not missed on the Wing, for her

absence could be nothing but a relief. But she had gained a kind of immortality for she had become part of the prison vocabulary and in years to come an officer could be heard saying, 'We must watch out for so and so or she'll do a Lily Hever on us.'

Which is a kind of fame, and one which Lily herself would have appreciated.

CHAPTER TEN

Christmas is always a difficult time in prison. Those of the inmates who are not missing their families miss their locals and their drinking cronies. Those who are about to be discharged are deeply resentful that their discharge hasn't come a week or two earlier; whilst those who have only just come in are even more depressed and resentful than the average new admission.

At Stone Park, the staff (and the prison visitors) do what they can to create a Christmas spirit. The 'Friends of Stone Park' provide Christmas cards for anyone who has none from outside. Decorations go up, rules are relaxed, and every woman is given a little more money to spend in the shop. An extra film show and a concert party are given. Many little parties are held, some arranged by the officers and some by the women themselves. Even Chef holds one in the kitchen for his workers.

Old Lizzie was in her glory, holding select little têtes-à-tête in her cell, and constantly sending one of the younger screws to fetch her 'some boiling water dear to make a nice cuppa for my friend.' Lizzie was greatly privileged being allowed her own tea set, which she kept in her locker and guarded with her life.

For Faye (and for the officers) Christmas was a time of strain. Those who were married had their own families to look after and plan for, while at the same time having to do more for their charges. And as always, Christmas was succeeded by a blank sense of anticlimax and boredom.

One afternoon in the New Year Mrs Armitage arrived home feeling very tired. She took off the coat of her suit and was about to drop it on the settee, when habit proved too strong for her and she hung it neatly over a chair. She sighed. Ted Armitage came in from the kitchen. He had been intended by nature to be a big man but years of suffering had shrunk him, leaving a frame on which his clothes hung loosely. He walked awkwardly using two sticks. His face too bore the marks of pain and he had querulous lines round his mouth. But his eyes were kind and patient. He led the life of a recluse, doing the lighter chores, watching television and always waiting for his wife to get home.

He smiled now, as he saw that she was back.

'Hullo love,' he said. 'You're late. I've made you a cup of coffee.'

'Thanks Ted. I'll take the weight off my feet for a bit.' She sat with a grunt of relief, and took off her sensible, somewhat large shoes.

'That's better.'

She drank her coffee, thankful to be able to relax.

'What kind of day?' asked Ted.

'Oh, the usual. Short staffed, a lot of officers out on escort duty.' She paused. 'Mrs Weekes is back with tonight's intake. Remember her? Old Georgie Weekes. Madam will be quite upset to see her. She thought she was out for good.'

'I can imagine that. She's very like you, your Mrs Boswell.'

'Like me?' Mrs Armitage sounded incredulous.

'Yes. She minds what happens to 'em.'

'Then she shouldn't show it so plainly,' said his wife shortly.

'More coffee?'

'Later.' She looked at him. 'What is it Ted? You've got something on your mind.'

He lowered himself into a specially high built chair and sat with his sticks on either side.

'Molly,' he said. 'Our Ellen was here today.'

The Chief's face tightened.

'Oh,' she said.

'She brought the child with her.'

'Did she now?'

'Little Samantha.'

'Ridiculous name.'

'It's fashionable, Ellen says. She's a pretty little girl and bright for two. I wish you could see her.'

'How can I if Ellen comes when I'm out? And it's not the first time is it? She's been here once or twice recently hasn't she?'

'How did you know?'

'From the way you talked about her, things you let drop.'

'It's been nearly three years since she left home.'

Mrs Armitage put down her cup with a bang. When she spoke again her voice was hard.

'So my daughter chooses to visit when she knows I won't be at home.'

'She only comes when you're out because she's afraid you wouldn't welcome her.'

There was no reply to this.

'Is she still living with that man?'

'Yes.'

'Are they married yet?'

'No.'

'Then I stand by what I've always said. I won't see her or the child.'

'Our grand daughter.' Ted sounded wistful.

'Her child,' snapped his wife. 'Nothing to do with me. She only had it to spite us.'

She got up abruptly and stood looking out of the window. With some courage Ted spoke again. For a man who is almost entirely dependent on his wife in every sense, it takes courage to speak his mind. But he was determined to try and ease the situation between mother and daughter.

'Look love,' he began. 'I must say this. When we found out she was pregnant you were so terribly upset. But it wasn't the end of the world. It happens all the time. If we'd been a bit more understanding she wouldn't have left home.'

'Nonsense. She wanted to leave home.' Mrs Armitage was visibly distressed. 'She stood in that door and told me she hated me. She said that she was going to live with that – that layabout just to show me what she thought of everything I stood for. She laughed at the way I brought her up.'

'She didn't mean it.' Ted Armitage spoke without conviction.

'Then it's for her to prove that.'

Ted shook his head. The situation was almost too difficult to cope with. Ellen was, in her own way, as pig headed as her mother. He must try another tack.

'You're so reasonable and understanding with the prisoners. Why can't you be the same with your own daughter?'

Mrs Armitage turned round and stared at him. Then she went quickly to her bedroom and shut the door. Ted made his way to it and stood listening. Then inside he heard muffled sobs. From Molly, Molly who never cried!

'I must let her get over this by herself,' he thought, and sat down to write a letter to his daughter.

Mrs Armitage was right. Faye was distressed when she heard Mrs Weekes was again within these walls. She was a nice old woman of a breed which no longer exists. She had two weaknesses, drink and petty shoplifting. Last time she had been in, Faye had had a long talk with her before she was discharged. She had even been to see her in the flat where Mrs Weekes looked after her invalid sister. She had been impressed by the way Mrs Weekes was coping, and had felt convinced that this would be the last Stone Park would see of her. So why, she wondered, was the old lady back again?

She had heard the news in the Centre where she and Mrs

Armitage had paused to look at the books of reports and applications.

Charles Radley came up to them, carrying folders with details of the new inmates.

'Guess who's back?'

'If you mean Mrs Weekes, I saw her last night,' said the Chief.

'Mrs Weekes!' Faye's voice was sharp with surprise.

'Yes, madam, she came in with last night's intake.'

'She's been on a bender, so she went into hospital for the night. Sister says she's better this morning,' said Radley.

'Oh dear, I thought she'd got over the drinking. She seemed so content, and the flat was really nice.'

The Chief said, 'How long has she got this time, Mr Radley?'

'Twelve months. Quite a lot at her age. Six months each on two counts. The Court had no alternative. She ran amok in the China Department of the local big store. Did hundreds of pounds worth of damage. It took two policemen to grab her and she bit one of them so badly that he had to go to Casualty. Of course she was stoned out of her mind at the time.'

Faye was astonished. 'It sounds quite unlike Mrs Weekes. Will you take the new admissions, Charles? I'll see her alone later. There must be something behind this.'

She went on up to her room. Mrs Armitage looked after her.

'She's never learnt. Never will,' she said with a little shake of her head.

'What d'you mean?' said Radley.

'You try to help them but you mustn't expect them not to let you down. You can't trust any of them.'

Privately Charles Radley agreed with her. But he did not say so.

About an hour later Sister Baxter came to Faye with a written report sheet.

'The medical report on Mrs Weekes, madam.'

'Thanks. How is she?'

'Not too bad considering. She's been on a bad drinking bout and also she'd been sleeping rough the night before she came in.'

'I just can't understand it. She lived in such a nice flat.'

'Anyhow Dr Mayes says she'll be quite all right to go on one of the Wings. We're short of beds at the moment.'

Faye was looking at the report.

'They only picked her up yesterday?'

'Yes. I believe they took her straight to the Magistrates Court and they gave her the maximum.'

'I see. Did you bring her up?'

'Yes. The Chief said you wanted to see her.'

'Bring her in will you?'

Faye glanced again at the report; and then Sister Baxter came in again with Mrs Weekes.

'Thank you Sister. You'll want to get back I suppose, so don't wait.'

'Thank you madam.'

Sister shut the door, as Mrs Weekes, very diffident and hesitant came towards Faye's desk. She was quite well dressed, but there was a split in the blouse of her suit, and a cut on her cheek. She looked white and somewhat trembly. She gave one of her little bobs.

'Weekes, Georgina. Sorry m'm, but I don't know me new number.'

'That's all right Mrs Weekes. You'd better sit down.' Mrs Weekes looked round and sat on the most uncomfortable chair she could see. 'I don't know what to say about all this. I never expected to see you in here again. You were managing so beautifully.'

'Yes m'm. I never touched a drop m'm. I'd given it up.'

'I know.'

Mrs Weekes gave an unhappy sniff.

'Who's going to look after your sister now?'

There was a pause. Mrs Weekes seemed on the verge of tears. With an effort she controlled herself. When she spoke her voice was very quiet.

'She's dead m'm. Poor old Jess. She just went to sleep and never woke up again. Lovely for her. But it was a shock to me. The young woman from the Welfare was kind, came and helped me with the funeral arrangements and all. She came to the funeral too and so did our neighbours next door. But she couldn't come home with me and when I got back . . .' her voice broke '. . . somebody had broken in. I rang the police. It was kids, they said, just kids did it. They'd smashed everything up, poured the milk and the tea on the floor and on the bed – they'd done things you wouldn't believe – dirty it was, horrible. I couldn't even start to clean it up. They'd stole a lot too, the telly had gone.'

'How horrible for you.' Faye remembered the neat if overcrowded little flat and was deeply sympathetic. 'What did you do?' But she thought she knew the answer.

'I went out and had a nip just to steady meself. A glass of gin it was – then another – and another. First time for over a year. Then it was too late to stop. I met up with some woman and we went on drinking. Slept in some cellar I think. Can't remember much about it. The next morning, I didn't know where to turn. . .' Mrs Weekes paused.

'So you went and broke up the things in that shop.'

'I suppose I did m'm. I was so wild – over me little home – I couldn't stop meself.'

'Oh I think you could, Mrs Weekes. I think you knew exactly what you were doing.'

Mrs Weekes gazed at her. Faye spoke gently.

'Why did you want to come back to prison?'

For a moment Mrs Weekes did not speak. Then she decided to come clean.

'I'd nowhere else to go. Jess has gone. The flat's smashed

up. Outside there's nothing for me now. In 'ere, nobody expects nothing of you. And I couldn't bear to think of being alone again.'

Faye looked as severe as she could. 'You're an old fraud,' she said. 'Is the flat locked up now?'

'Yes'm. The police put on a padlock.'

'Good. I'll send Miss Clarke to see you and take all the details. She'll arrange to have it all tidied up for you. By the way, did you tell them about this in Court yesterday?'

'No'm. I forgot.'

'I bet you did, you dear old humbug,' thought Faye, and called in the officer who was waiting outside and told her to take Mrs Weekes to North Wing.

On the way, Mrs Weekes who was beginning to feel much better, asked Officer Dudgeon who was escorting her, whether it was still that nice Miss Harker. And Miss Dudgeon replied that it was.

'That's nice,' said Mrs Weekes. 'I like North Wing.'

She greeted Janet Harker with enthusiasm.

'I'm ever so glad I got on your Wing, Miss,' she said. 'I was afraid I might have got Miss Parrish. It's ever so much nicer here.'

'We aim to please,' said Janet wickedly, and Pat Berryman turned away to hide a splutter of laughter. 'By the way,' Janet added, 'there's a friend of yours still here. Old Lizzie.'

'Lizzie?' Mrs Weekes face lit up. 'That's nice. When you've given me me cell and me number, I'll go and pass the time of day with her.'

'You'll have to shout a bit. She's got very deaf,' said Janet, and proceeded to allocate a cell and a number to the prodigal returned.

When she had found her cell and unpacked her meagre belongings she set out to look for Lizzie, peering at the names on the cell doors. When she saw it, a broad smile broke over her face. She put her head round the open door. Lizzie was reading a magazine, mouthing the words silently, to herself.

'Lizzie,' said Mrs Weekes, and then louder, 'Lizzie!'

Lizzie heard her the second time and looked up. For a moment she did not see who it was: and then she recognised her old friend.

'Georgie Weekes!' she said.

The two old women beamed at each other.

Lizzie put out her hands and Mrs Weekes grasped them.

'Why!' said Lizzie. 'I thought you was out. They said you'd gone straight.'

Mrs Weekes grinned. 'I had but . . . but Jess died and things went wrong. Hate being on me own. Glad to be back. How are you keeping, Lizzie?'

'Can't complain. Me indigestion's a bother. At my age there's bound to be something. Come on in, sit down.' She patted the bed. 'I only lets the very best sit on that, the Governor and you.'

Mrs Weekes touched the quilt gingerly as she admired it.

'It's beautiful,' she said.

'That's what Madam said. All me own work.'

'You're lucky, 'aving your own things.'

'I'll make you a pot of tea,' said old Lizzie, showing off a bit.

'*A pot of tea?*' Mrs Weekes couldn't believe it.

'I always 'av the makings,' replied Lizzie proudly. She opened her locker and took out a white table cloth with a deep crochet edge. She laid it on the table. Then out of the locker came an old fashioned flower china tea-pot, and cups and saucers to match. Mrs Weekes was speechless; and Lizzie saw this with delight.

'You just stay where you are Georgie. I'll get one of the screws to put the kettle on.'

Five minutes later the two old ladies were sitting sipping their tea, and enjoying a gossip.

'D'you like watching telly Lizzie?' asked Mrs Weekes.

Lizzie shook her head firmly. 'Can't hear it. Don't want to look at it either. Lot of Yanks shooting at each other and girls showing their belly-buttons. Never could stand belly-buttons.' They both giggled delightedly.

'D'you remember that dark haired brass who used to stand up on the old windowsill, that big window in the old wash-house. What *was* her name?'

Lizzie delved into her memories of the past.

'Mavis. Mavis Taplow.'

'Topham,' said Weekes.

'That's what I said,' answered Lizzie. 'Taplow. Pulled up her skirts she used to. There she stood showing herself to the men on the working parties.'

'She had a nerve,' said Mrs Weekes laughing.

'They was laying the drains for K block. There was one little Welshman,' said Lizzie. 'Oh he was a corker! I could have done with a bit.'

'You were a one, Lizzie. When would that have been?'

'Must have been just before the war, the old washhouse has gone now.'

'It's all changed.' Mrs Weekes voice was regretful.

'No uniforms. It's all wrong. Some of these girls look right nits, all them trousers,' said Lizzie.

'You heard the latest?' said Mrs Weekes. 'I saw it in the paper. The new prison is all arranged for nut cases, nothing but. Those at the top say any woman in here must be soft in the head.'

'Rubbish,' said Lizzie. 'They don't know what they're at.' She lowered her voice. 'What d'you think of the Governor Georgie?'

'She's been good to me Lizzie.'

'M'm. She's all right. But if you ask me, she's a sight too good looking for a Governor.'

* * *

Mrs Armitage was in a very bad temper. She had come to ask the Governor a favour, and it had been refused. She had wanted to cut down the amount of time the women spent in free association on the following day.

'Why?' asked Faye, surprised. 'It's little enough as it is.'

'This is why, madam.' And Mrs Armitage handed her a list of the officers who would be away on escort duty the next day.

Faye read it. 'But it's nearly two thirds of your staff,' she said.

'Exactly. I've barely enough of them left to supervise working parties, meals and applications. If the women see the officers are a bit thin on the ground, it's asking for trouble.'

'But if we went back to the old system of locking them up more, that would lead to trouble too.' Faye sounded very firm. 'By all means postpone non-essential classes tomorrow. But I can't agree to an earlier lock up or anything like that.'

'Very well, madam,' said the Chief, very stiffly indeed. She turned to go.

'Naturally, if anything goes wrong, it will be my responsibility,' said Faye.

'Of course, madam.' With disapproval written in every line of her face, Mrs Armitage left.

When she got back to North Wing she was in a bad temper. Without asking Janet, she picked up the Duty Roster in a snappish sort of way.

'Spencer will have to go on late duty tomorrow night,' she said in her abrupt manner.

'She's had a bit more than her share lately,' said Janet. 'She won't like it.'

'No-one likes it, Miss Harker. But while we are so understaffed, we all have to put ourselves out.'

Janet opened her mouth to say something, decided against it and shut it again.

'You realize, don't you, how many officers will be away

tomorrow?' Mrs Armitage was still riding her favourite hobby horse.

Fortunately the telephone rang. Janet answered it, and passed it to the Chief, who took it. 'Hallo,' she said. 'What is it? Didn't he say more? Very well.'

She hung up looking perturbed. 'My husband rang. He said it was urgent. Something serious has happened.'

'Perhaps you'd better get home.'

'Sure you can cope?'

'Of course.'

'Then I think I will. I'll make up the two hours tomorrow, any road.'

Outside the prison she hailed a taxi, an unprecedented extravagence for her, but the buses were crowded at this time of day and she was on tenterhooks to get home in case Ted had fallen again, as he had before Christmas. Fortunately, both for her purse and her peace of mind, it was only a short way and she reached her home in less than ten minutes. She hurried up the stairs to her second floor flat, her key in her hand and opened the front door.

'Ted,' she called anxiously. 'Where are you? Are you all right?'

She looked up to see her husband standing in the kitchen door. He looked a little tense but perfectly well.

'What's wrong? They said it was serious.' Like a mother who beats a child who has just not been run over, Mrs Armitage now sounded furious with him. 'I thought something had happened to you.'

Ted Armitage was nerving himself to speak.

'As a matter of fact,' he said, in a tentative way. 'The fact is – Ellen's here.'

'Ellen!' Mrs Armitage sounded angrier than ever. 'I thought you'd fallen or hurt yourself. I was told it was urgent.'

'It is urgent. They're moving up North. They may not be back for years. And I wanted you and Ellen to see each other.'

A girl appeared in the doorway of the kitchen. She was not unattractive, with fine eyes: intelligent looking though rather intense. Her clothes were old and resolutely unsmart. Mrs Armitage looked up and then, quickly, looked away.

Muttering 'I'll leave you together,' Ted went into the kitchen.

Ellen advanced further into the room. 'He wanted us to meet,' she said. 'I told him I'd see you if you came now.'

'Good of you.' Her mother's voice was biting.

'I didn't realise you didn't know I was here,' said Ellen. 'I thought – if you'd take a couple of hours off work to come and see me it might prove something – not much, but – something.'

Mrs Armitage would not look at her. 'I've never refused to see you,' she said.

'As long as it was on your terms.'

'*My* terms? It was you that walked out.'

Ellen checked herself. 'Dad's looking better. I was really worried over him when he had that fall before Christmas. But now he seems fine.'

'Yes, he's got over it remarkably well.' Like Ellen Mrs Armitage was trying hard to be reasonable. 'He's so good. Never complains. Just now, I was worried to death. I thought he'd had another fall.'

'It wasn't my fault he didn't say I was here,' said Ellen.

'I didn't say it was. What are you doing now? Still nursing?'

'No. I'm doing social work with the St Pancras Community. The homeless, addicts and so on.'

'I know the sort.' Her tone spoke volumes. 'What's this about you going up North?'

'Lenny's applied for a job as assistant textile designer in a factory near Carlisle.'

'When will you leave?'

'In two or three weeks, if he gets the job.'

'*If.*' The moment her mother had said this, she regretted it.

And Ellen jumped in on it. 'What d'you mean *if*?'

'He hasn't exactly had conspicuous success with his jobs has he?'

Ellen was rapidly losing her temper. 'He's a brilliant artist,' she said hotly. 'He could take his pick of a hundred jobs!'

'Then why doesn't he, instead of living off you and the Welfare?'

'What's it got to do with you anyway?'

They were by now, both of them, past the point of no return.

'I'm your mother,' said Mrs Armitage furiously.

'That doesn't give you any right to judge me by your own petty, reactionary standards.'

'Don't talk to me like that, my girl.'

'I'm not your girl. And I'm not some frightened prisoner locked up in your lousy jail.'

Mrs Armitage made a quick movement towards her.

'What are you going to do? Hit me? You'd enjoy that, wouldn't you?' said Ellen furiously.

Just in time Mr Armitage appeared in the kitchen doorway.

'Ellen,' he pleaded. 'Be careful what you say to your mother.'

Ellen turned to him. 'I'm leaving, Dad. You're married to her. You have to take it. I don't.' She turned to her mother. 'I should have known better than to expect anything from you. You've never shown me any affection before; why should I expect any now? All I was to you was an unpaid skivvy.

When I remember how we lived, like another Wing in your prison!'

'Don't try and justify yourself. You remember only what you want to.'

'I remember how I was brought up. Rules, rules; do this, do that. The other kids laughed at me. "Your mum's a screw," they used to say.'

'And proud of it,' said Mrs Armitage stoutly.

'I bet you are! Proud of the whole rotten system!'

Ted Armitage came forward on his sticks. 'I won't let you talk to your mother like this. You've no idea how much she did for both of us.'

Ellen went to him and kissed him. 'Sorry, Dad. Of course you've got to stick up for her. But not me. Thank God I can give my own child some love. I'll make damn sure she's not brought up like I was.'

And she stormed out, without a backward look at her mother, slamming the front door behind her. Mrs Armitage looked bleakly at her husband. After a moment she went to the fireplace. On a shelf over the electric fire was a framed photograph of Ellen as a smiling little girl. For a moment she looked at it. When she spoke her voice was low.

'I know I must have seemed hard when she was a child,' she said. 'I wasn't really. It was just – she was so pretty. I was afraid of spoiling her. I wanted her to grow up to be a credit to us.'

'She didn't mean half the things she said just now.'

'She meant them all right. It's my own fault. I was too strict.'

She was not a woman who cried easily. But at this moment she was very near it. Her husband put his hand on her arm.

'I won't have you blaming yourself, Molly. When I had that accident we wouldn't have survived but for you. You took that job at the prison. You had to work damned hard, all hours. And look after a sick man and a child at the same time. I don't know how you stood it. You kept us all going.'

'I couldn't have unless I'd organised everything. And when Ellen got older I hoped she'd help me. But she didn't want to. What did I do wrong, Ted?'

'Maybe you should have trusted her more, let her make her own friends. She had no friends of her own till she started nursing.'

'I should have done things differently. I wish I had. But it's too late now. We've nothing in common and she hates me. And I can't change.'

'I wouldn't want you to. She had no call to speak to you like that.'

There was a pause.

'I think she had. I suppose every child needs love and I had no time to give it. And now I wouldn't know how. Except for you. I know how they see me at Stone Park, most of 'em. Rigid, humourless and hard. And that's how Ellen sees me. She's on one side of the fence and I'm on the other. And there's no way through.'

There was a pause before Ted Armitage spoke.

'You do love her, Molly, but you don't know how to show it. Look, she brought this for you, hoping to make things up.'

He handed his wife an envelope. In it was a blown-up snapshot of Ellen's child.

Mrs Armitage looked at it stonily. Then: 'She's pretty enough. But just look at those jeans. They need mending. But Ellen was always a bit of a slut.' She rose and put the snapshot alongside the one of Ellen. Then she turned to her husband.

'I'll get some coffee. And next time your daughter calls, Ted Armitage, I'd be obliged if you wouldn't drag me home for no reason whatever.'

Mrs Armitage was back to her usual form again.

CHAPTER ELEVEN

The following Sunday was a gloomy monochrome day outside, but the sitting room of the Boswell's house was very peaceful. Bill was dozing in his armchair. The fire had sunk rather low: from its depths came a deep red glow. Out of doors the grey rain poured down. Faye herself was resting on the sofa. The room was comfortably untidy. The Sunday papers were strewn about the floor and Bill, who had been sorting his records before lunch, had not yet finished them, and the covers lay scattered. Faye, an orderly woman, would normally have found this irritating. But today she felt relaxed and comfortable and enjoyed the easy sprawling atmosphere.

Today's laziness was a bonus. She and Bill had been going to Sussex to spend the day with one of Bill's more boring associates, but when they woke the rain was already pouring down, and the weathermen promised no let up. It was Bill who had rung and, making a plausible excuse, had put off their planned visit. It had been a totally unexpected rest for Faye and one which she needed, for the last two weeks had been particularly fraught.

She yawned and stretched herself luxurously. She had not even thought of Stone Park for several hours.

Yesterday she and Bill had had a short letter from Paul who had been in Bangladesh for over a year. She picked it up and read it again. 'Dear Ma and Bill,' he wrote, 'I have decided what I want to do with my life. To go back to England despite the inflation and general gloom, perhaps because of it. And I have decided what I want to do, which is to train as a Probation Officer. My motto being, prison never did anyone any good, so for God's sake let's keep as many people out as possible. I expect you'll be sorry, Bill, that I am going into such a badly paid profession. But ma will understand, I guess, and will no doubt be pleased if I do take some of her potential customers away. So get that secretary girl of yours to post me all the bumf she can find about training schedules and the like. I aim to leave here in September.

It will be marvellous to see my dear old boat again. Not so bad to see my dear old parents, too.

Love to you both. Don't work too hard, Ma. How is your waistline Bill? Bless you. Paul.'

Faye had missed Paul during the past year and thought with pleasure of having him home again. The faint snoring from Bill's chair had stopped, and looking up she saw that he had woken and was smiling at her.

'It will be fine to have him home again,' he said.

'Yes,' said Faye. 'He got a good degree,' (Paul had read sociology). 'Now it won't be wasted.'

Bill got up and put on a recording of the Eroica. When Paul gets home, thought Faye, it won't only be Beethoven, and then realized that probably Paul would want to go and live on his own. She and Bill sat in companionable silence until he said: 'Mind if we talk about me for once?'

'Darling,' said Faye, 'what a pig you make me sound.'

'Not a pig at all. Just a very busy lady whom I happen to be privileged to be married to.'

He smiled at her and said: 'What would you say if I was retired from the business?'

Faye was so surprised that she sat bolt upright and more newspapers slid off her lap. 'Darling, what do you mean? I can't imagine you doing nothing.'

'I didn't say I was going to do nothing. I've got plans. But there are younger men coming up, so it seems only fair to make way for them. It would mean I wouldn't be out of England nearly so much. What would you think of that?'

'I think it would be wonderful.' They looked at each other. Faye realised she would feel an overwhelming relief: although she had never mentioned it to Bill, she had felt uneasy ever since the hijacking, and found that when he was away she was not sleeping well.

He leant across and patted her hand. He knew her so well that there was no need for her to put her thoughts into words.

'I may have news for you soon,' he said.

The telephone rang. It was Janet Harker ringing from Stone Park, very apologetic at disturbing Faye on a Sunday. She had mislaid Cecily Foyle's number and wondered if Faye had it as she knew they were personal friends. Faye gave it to her and asked if everything was all right. For a few moments they chatted; then Faye rang off.

'She's a nice girl,' said Bill. 'What's happened about her marriage to that young doctor?'

'Richard? I'm afraid it's not going to happen. Not just yet, at least. He's going to Bristol for three years and wants her to leave Stone Park.'

'And she won't?'

'No.'

'Pity. He seemed a nice chap,' said Bill.

'He is. And they're so well suited to each other. But I can see her point. She's doing such good work and to have to throw it up. . . .'

'You mean that he should have thrown up his new job in order to let her stay on?' said Bill dryly.

Faye felt they were on dangerous ground. She refused to be drawn into an argument and only said 'They are so good together that I can't help feeling that it will all come right in the end.' And in order to turn away from a dangerous corner she added. 'We ought to have the Radleys in one evening. It won't be so easy once the baby arrives.'

'When is that?'

'Quite soon. I don't know what Charles will do if it's a girl. He talks about "Crispin" all the time. It's extraordinary how this has changed him. He used not to be a home man at all, but now he can't wait to get back to Beth.'

'You and he don't agree as well as you used to, do you?'

'Why do you say that?' Faye asked.

Bill shrugged. 'You used to say that he always backed you up, however radical your ideas were. But now I get the impression that this isn't so.'

'He's always completely loyal to me publicly, but I must admit that in private we have had some heated arguments lately. Sometimes I think he should go back to a men's prison.'

'You think he finds the women unbearable?'

'Not the inmates. But I and the staff and the welfare people do irritate him; he thinks we are all too emotional, and apt to sentimentalise situations.'

Bill smiled. 'He's probably right. He'd better apply for a Governorship of a male prison next time one comes up. And good luck to him. All the same, I don't mind betting the baby's a girl.'

Bill would have lost his bet, for when the baby arrived, right on time, it was a boy. It was a normal and easy birth.

Charles was ecstatic when he was first shown the little object. Beth privately thought that the baby looked like a very old and furious Eskimo but did not tell her husband this. Within a few days both she and the baby were at home again to the delight of Charles: a delight tempered by the fact that Beth's mother had come to stay for a week or two. She was an extremely capable woman, and like many capable women, very bossy. She and her son-in-law did not respond to each other. She had an irritating way of referring to Stone Park as 'that dreadful place where Charles works'. He sometimes felt that she regarded him as though he were a criminal himself. During her visit he took the opportunity of working after supper, taking a lot of paper work into his study. He remembered how this had been a habit of his for years, a habit he had now given up. How boring it must have been for Beth, he thought. No wonder our marriage nearly foundered. Still, all things come to an end, as did his mother-in-law's visit.

On the evening she left, after supper, which he had insisted on washing up, he looked with great affection at Beth. Motherhood suited her, she was looking very handsome. The strain of the past few years had entirely left her face. She smiled at her husband.

'It's nice to be alone,' said Charles and added hastily. 'Not that I wasn't very grateful to your mother.'

'You should be,' said Beth with a smile. 'She gave us fourteen unbroken nights.'

A pause while Charles digested this.

'You mean – the baby cries?'

'Yes. Every night. About two o'clock, mother said.'

'Is there anything wrong with him?' asked Charles, instantly anxious.

'No. The clinic says he's a hungry baby and they do cry sometimes.'

'Why doesn't he cry in the daytime?'

'I don't know. I wish he would. But he keeps it for the nights.'

They both looked into the carrycot where the baby slept, angelically. He was now less like an ancient Eskimo and was growing daily into a cherub. The parents looked at him, transfixed by the beauty of their handiwork. Then they smiled at each other, ruefully.

'We're a bit old to start this lark,' Beth said. 'We should have done it ten years ago. We mustn't be over-anxious parents, darling.'

'No,' said Charles, 'we mustn't. Of course not. All the same I'll have a word with Peter Mayes. He'll know about this crying business and can give us some advice.'

* * *

One evening a month or two after this, Faye was finishing some paperwork in her office. Peter Mayes was with her. He had been working off the stress of the day; and Radley, who had come in to give Faye some reports he had had from the Home Office, was listening to him with some amusement.

'After a day spent with our uncommunicative or retarded clients, it's a blessed relief to talk to someone sane,' Peter Mayes was saying.

'I'm afraid I haven't contributed much to the conversation,' said Faye, who was still signing letters.

'Silent, sympathetic, understanding,' said Radley.

Faye laughed. 'Give me a drink,' she said. 'And yourselves too.'

Radley proceeded to do so.

'You see,' said Mayes. 'I can't talk to my old friend here any more. He doesn't listen. He's only interested in potty training and the like. He was round again this morning asking advice about the baby crying at night.'

'I'm not surprised,' said Faye with a twinkle. 'We had a staff meeting this morning and the poor dear dozed off, didn't you Charles? Never mind, it's only a phase: it won't go on for long, will it, Peter?'

'Not when the baby is as healthy a specimen as Master Crispin,' said Peter Mayes. 'Still, I miss our sessions in the pub after work. It's off home to change the nappies, eh Charles?'

'Well yes, I do change him.' Both the others laughed. 'After all Beth has him all day, it's only right I should take over for a bit in the evening.'

'Heaven preserve me from matrimony,' said the doctor. But Faye didn't think he said it with conviction. She put down her pen and looked at him.

'You know, Peter,' she said, 'I worry about you. It's not like you to be so openly cynical.'

'Openly?'

'Wide open,' said Radley. 'You've been beefing for the last month.'

'Have I?' asked the doctor, and added, more seriously. 'Perhaps it is because you two are practising your profession, while I have become a dispenser of nostrums. I'm so taken up with routine, I have no time for any research. I dole out the same old pills, listen to the same old complaints, knowing that at least half of them are faked in order to get off work.'

' "Skivers", as the Chief would say,' said Faye.

'Exactly. While anything remotely interesting or unusual is whisked away to one of the London hospitals. But you mustn't pay any attention to me, I've simply been at the grindstone for too long.'

'Far be it for me to make a diagnosis, but I'd say you had a touch of a disease we all have to watch out for in this place – a kind of mental claustrophobia.'

'Institutionalisation,' said Radley.

'Inst . . .' Mayes smiled. 'I can't even say it. Don't fash yourself. I just need a drink or two.'

'Let's go across to the pub now,' said Radley.

'What about the nappies?' said Mayes.

'If you ask me, Beth will be rather relieved not to have me flapping around for a change. I'll ring her before we leave. Come along to my office now; I can see that Faye wants to get on with her work.'

Left to herself, Faye worked steadily through the file of reports which Mr Morton had left for her to approve and sign. She had almost finished them when there was a knock on her door. It was Miss Clarke.

'Can you spare a minute?' she asked.

'Of course. Come and sit down. Any worries?'

'What do you think?' Miss Clarke smiled. 'But today, two in particular.'

'Which are?'

'Firstly, Mrs Armitage.'

Faye was so surprised that she took off her spectacles and blinked.

'What on earth. . . .'

'Simply that I'm really concerned, she seems so fearfully snappy and disagreeable; I know she's always been a strict disciplinarian but now she's gone too far. If she isn't careful she'll be giving the inmates a real grievance. And what is worse, she's getting on the wrong side of the officers.'

'I've noticed it too,' said Faye. 'I've tried to talk to her, tactfully, to find out what's troubling her, but it's not the slightest use.'

'You've met her husband, haven't you?'

'Yes. . . .'

'D'you know, I believe you're the only person of the entire staff who has been asked inside her doors – except Martha Parrish of course.'

Faye laughed. 'It was hardly a social visit. There had been some crisis. I remember now, it was the night Lily Hever died, and we were so late getting away that I insisted on driving her home. And I suppose she felt she could not help asking me in for a cup of coffee.'

'What is he like?'

'Nature meant him to be a tough big man, a typical Prison Officer. Years of illness and pain have turned him into a thin rather tetchy saint. He obviously adores her. There was a photograph of their wedding. She was a most attractive young woman. There's a daughter, I believe; he said something about it, whilst the Chief was in the kitchen making coffee. But he shut up like a clam when she came back.'

'Perhaps the daughter died?'

'That shouldn't make her disagreeable. Regretful, yes, but not cross.'

Faye knew what she was talking about. Her own daughter

had been killed while riding her bicycle on her tenth birthday.

Liz Clarke remembered this.

'Oh, I am sorry,' she exclaimed. 'How tactless of me.'

'Don't be,' said Faye. 'Not tactless at all. Anyhow, I will have a word with Martha Parrish and see if she knows what it's all about. You're perfectly right, she can't go on as she is at present.'

There was a gentle knock on the door. It was Cecily Foyle who looked less than her usual cheerful self.

'Can you spare a second?' she said.

'Come in and sit down. You look worried.'

'I am worried. I've been to see Vivien. It's pointless. She's really not there at all. We used to get on so well and now she seems positively to dislike me.'

Faye sighed. 'I'm afraid she dislikes everyone and everything now. One can't really blame the girl. Life has played a pretty dirty trick on her. And it can't help, to know that it was entirely her own fault.'

'For falling in love with that wretched man?'

'Exactly.'

'If only one could give her an interest. She's got a good brain. Couldn't she use it in some way? Get a degree or something?'

Faye paused before answering. 'There's a condition many of the long term prisoners reach, when rehabilitation is no longer possible and they can only move down hill.'

'The older officers call it gaol rot,' said Miss Clarke.

'How horrible,' said Cecily.

'For some reason, partly from the shocks she has had to take, partly because she was so near to release, Vivien has reached this state very quickly,' said Faye.

And Miss Clarke added. 'And I fear there is very little we can do about it.'

'It sounds pretty depressing,' said Cecily.

'I know it is. But one must realise that for some of the

prisoners there is no fairy tale happy ending. And Vivien's one of them.'

'What do the head shrinkers say?' Cecily was referring somewhat disparagingly to Faye's rapidly swelling staff of trained psychiatrists, a body of eager young men and women, most of them fresh from university, and all of them very conscious of their own importance in the scheme of things.

'Oh, they submit long and for the most part, totally incomprehensible reports,' said Faye. And then, feeling she was on dangerous ground, she turned to Miss Clarke and said:

'What was the other thing that was worrying you?'

'Well, it isn't really a worry. Something rather nice.'

'Thank heaven for that,' thought Faye. It had been a depressing day on the whole and some good news would not come amiss.

'What is it?' she asked.

'Sandra Logan.'

'The girl with the crying baby?' said Cecily.

'Yes. Only it's stopped crying now. I had to go to K block to see about those coloured twins going into Care, and Sister called me into her office. Apparently Sandra has found herself a suitor.'

'Where and how?' asked Faye.

'Some time after Easter. You remember what lovely weather it was, quite warm, and Sister let the mothers go into the garden with their babies. Two of the maintenance men were working on the outside, and apparently the younger one fell for Sandra. Sister says he's a nice fella, a painter by trade and he's perfectly serious about the girl.'

'Does he know the baby's illegitimate?' asked Faye.

'Yes, and is prepared to bring it up as his own.'

'And Sandra?'

'She's actually woken up and is talking quite a lot, planning her wedding dress. She had some money saved.'

'When is she due for discharge?'

'On May 29th, and the wedding is to be on the 30th.'

'Well!' said Faye. 'Cecily, there's a fairy tale ending for you.'

'Yes I suppose it is. All the same Sandra was rather a stupid girl.'

'But a very pretty one,' said Faye. 'She'll probably be a perfectly satisfactory wife.'

Soon after this Faye's two visitors departed and she turned to the last two reports. She had just finished reading them when there was another knock on the door. This time it opened before Faye could answer and her husband came in.

'Why Bill. . . .'

Bill smiled. 'I thought we were going out for a meal, to celebrate my new career.'

'Sorry darling. I got held up by these reports. But now I've nearly finished. Give yourself a glass of sherry.'

She was tidying the reports on her desk as Bill fetched himself a drink. He looked round at the room on which Faye had by now imprinted so much of her own personality. The sofa which she had imported and the two modern lithographs, one David Hockney and one Francis Bacon. The large oil painting of a very early governor in her dark Victorian dress and severe hair could not, thought Bill, be a greater contrast to Faye.

'It's fascinating to see you in your natural habitat,' said Bill.

'Natural?' asked Faye.

'Well, most of your life is spent here now. Hasn't it become more important than our own home?'

Faye laughed. 'I hope not. I don't want the prison to take over my whole life. I was saying just now to Peter that we mustn't let ourselves become institutionalised. There! That's done at last.'

'What were they?' asked Bill.

'Half yearly reports for the Home Office, concerning practically every facet of prison life, from the number of toilet rolls used to the number of suicides. Mercifully the last item has been nil for the past half year.'

She got up. 'Give me five minutes to tidy up, darling, and then, off for a lovely dinner.'

CHAPTER TWELVE

The next day, as the women queued up for lunch, Mrs Armitage came onto the North Wing. She noticed an untidy pile of magazines which someone had left on one of the benches outside the cells.

'Get someone to clear that mess up, Mrs Spencer,' she said brusquely.

'I thought, after lunch,' said Mrs Spencer, who had lately been promoted to Principal Officer, and did not take kindly to being shouted at in public by the Chief.

'I said, get it cleared up,' snapped Mrs Armitage.

'Very well, Chief.' Mrs Spencer's lips were tightly compressed. Faye had been quite right in thinking that the officers would not stand for much more of this.

Old Lizzie and Mrs Weekes came out of Lizzie's cell and stood in the queue. Lizzie was very arthritic today and Mrs Weekes was helping her.

Just behind them was a very pretty innocent-looking girl, Jill, who was in for gross indecency. When they reached the pile of trays, she seemed to have some difficulty in holding hers. When she had filled it, she picked it up, and winced, as though her hands were hurting her. Suddenly the tray tipped forward and the dishes fell onto the floor. There was a chorus of shouts and jeers from the women, but Mrs Armitage topped them all.

'What's the matter?' she shouted accusingly to Jill. The girl looked scared. 'I couldn't hold it, Miss,' she said.

'Mrs Spencer, get this cleaned up.' The Chief's voice echoed across the Wing. 'The rest of you, keep moving.'

Mrs Spencer went across to Jill and gave her orders in a deliberately low voice.

Jill dropped onto her knees awkwardly picking up the plates and cutlery, while Mrs Weekes hurried forward to help her.

'I just couldn't hold it,' said Jill almost in tears.

'I'll help you dearie,' said Mrs Weekes.

They went into the washing recess where Mrs Weekes put away the plates and crockery to be washed up and Jill sprinkled some detergent into a bucket. She put her hand into the bucket to stir it and quickly took it out.

'What's the matter with your hands?' asked Mrs Weekes.

Jill held them out to her, soundlessly. They were both covered with an angry looking rash.

'That looks nasty. You better get it seen to.'

'How do I manage that?'

'You ask to see the doctor. I'll see to it for you if you like.'

'Thanks,' said Jill gratefully.

There was a roar from the entrance to the recess and both women jumped. It was, of course, Mrs Armitage.

'We haven't got all day. Get a move on.'

'It's her hands,' said Mrs Weekes. 'Ever such a bad rash.'

'No doubt,' said the Chief with heavy sarcasm. 'Take out a dustpan and clean up the mess.'

During this, the Governor had come onto the Wing, and had heard the stentorian tones of her Chief Officer. Janet Harker appeared in the doorway of her office; she looked at Faye; neither spoke, but each woman knew what the other was thinking.

Mrs Armitage turned away from the recess, shooing Jill and Mrs Weekes in front of her. She then turned and went towards the Governor.

'Anything wrong Mrs Armitage?'

'Nothing to speak of Madam. Just another skiver.' And muttering something about South Wing, she unlocked the door and went down the circular staircase.

'What is it, do you think?'

Janet shook her head. 'I don't know. It's been very bad the last few weeks.'

'Is everything all right at her home?'

Janet, usually a good-natured girl, reacted to this with some spirit.

'Other people have home worries without becoming impossible to work with.'

Faye knew what she was referring to. Janet's boyfriend had issued her an ultimatum. He was taking up his appointment in Bristol and wanted her to resign and go with him as his wife. But after serious thought she had realised that she could not give up her work, not yet anyhow. She had asked Faye's advice, who had told her to get married and possibly go back into the prison service later. But Janet had realised that Richard must accept the fact that she had loyalties too, and belief in the value of her work. So, sadly, they had separated. Sadly, for they were very much in love. Faye herself felt that they would marry eventually, and meantime she admired Janet for the way in which she had not allowed her own worries to affect her excellent work on the Wing. She smiled at her sympathetically. Then she said:

'In confidence, Janet, we will have to do something about the Chief. One of the troubles is that she hasn't had a real holiday; she's simply stayed at home and spring cleaned.'

'I know,' answered Janet. 'And working here, one does need to get right away once a year....'

When Mrs Weekes had finished helping Jill, she joined old Lizzie at the table, having fetched her own lunch first. Lizzie was not looking too well this morning. She was holding her arm across her chest, and there was pain in her face.

'You all right Lizzie?' asked her friend, concerned about her.

'It's me heartburn,' said Lizzie. She wasn't grumbling,

merely stating an inescapable fact. 'It's dreadful this morning.'

'You ought to go and see the doctor,' said Reba. 'That's what he's there for.'

'She's right Lizzie,' said Mrs Weekes.

Lizzie shook her head. 'I don't want to go making no trouble,' she said.

'It's not trouble,' answered Reba. 'It's their job. And that girl Jill ought to go and see about her hands.'

She and Mrs Weekes looked across to where Jill was sitting, eating her lunch and at intervals glancing at the palms of her hands in a worried sort of way.

'Yes,' said Mrs Weekes. 'That rash needs attention.'

'I don't want to go into the hospital,' said Lizzie. 'Leave all me things.'

'Maybe you wouldn't have to. He'd give you something to take,' said her friend. 'All the same I think you oughta see doctor. You make an application dear.'

Lizzie gave a gasp of pain and clutched her chest.

'There's the Chief,' said Reba, for indeed Mrs Armitage had just returned to the Wing. 'You go now dear,' she said to Mrs Weekes. 'Explain to the old cow what's happened,' and she added under her breath. 'If you ask me Lizzie looks real bad.'

Mrs Weekes got up unwillingly, for she too had experienced the rough side of the Chief's tongue during the past week. But she agreed with Reba that Lizzie didn't look well. Bravely she went up to Mrs Armitage.

'Could I have a word Chief?' she said.

'Well?' The Chief's tone was uncompromising.

'It's old Lizzie and that girl Jill: they want to see the doctor.'

Janet Harker stood listening.

'They know the Rules,' said the Chief. 'Tell them to make an application.'

'They want to go today.'

'Do they now.' Mrs Armitage sounded heavily sarcastic. 'Then they can wait till tomorrow.'

'But Lizzie looks bad,' said Mrs Weekes, 'and Jill's hands are paining her something awful.'

'She just wants to be excused work,' was the only answer she got from the Chief.

Janet felt it was time to intervene. 'If they want to see the doctor urgently, it is their right. And Lizzie isn't looking too good.'

'Anything for a bit of attention! Not to mention wasting time. I'll leave it to you Miss Harker. If it was my decision I'd let 'em wait.'

Janet, however, had different ideas and, having rung through to Peter Mayes, she arranged for Pat Berryman to take them along at three o'clock.

When they arrived (after a fairly slow journey, for Lizzie's arthritis was worrying her and she seemed a bit exhausted), Peter Mayes decided to see the young girl first, and told Berryman where she could find a comfortable chair for the old woman to rest in.

He took Jill into his surgery with Sister Baxter in attendance. Jill was very tense: she was afraid of doctors.

'Now,' said Peter Mayes. 'Let's look at these hands of yours.'

Shivering a little Jill held out her hands, palms upward. They were covered with an angry, faintly suppurating rash.

'H'm yes. That's fairly nasty. How long have you had it?'

Jill's voice was barely audible when she answered. 'Off and on, maybe two weeks.'

'Why didn't you come and see me before?'

'I thought it would go away. But today it started hurting real bad.'

Mayes smiled at her. He realised the girl was scared out of her mind. 'I'm not a bogey-man you know . . . you needn't be so scared. Have you ever had anything like this before?'

'No.'

'Where do you work?'

'In the kitchens. Washing up.'

'M'm. You've got a delicate skin, and I'd say the detergents haven't done it any good. D'you use disinfectants too?'

'Yes. For the sinks.'

'I'll give you some ointment and Sister will put on a dressing for you. Come back the day after tomorrow and we'll see how it goes. Will you see to it Sister? And tell Miss Berryman she is to be excused labour, till we see how it goes. Certainly no more kitchen work. Cheer up Jill.'

Jill summoned up a smile. He wasn't too bad, she thought. Treated you like a human being at least. And it was a relief to know that she needn't go back to that endless washing up. She was a model and had always taken care of her hands. She was in Stone Park because she had become involved in a kinky photographic session. She was twenty-two and slightly retarded, but she looked no more than a young seventeen. She sighed with pleasure as Sister worked in the soothing ointment. This was more like it. Nice to think she'd be back in a day or two. She looked at Sister's comfortable person and smiled again.

Meanwhile old Lizzie had been taken in to see the doctor. She was as usual very apologetic. 'I don't like to bother you, doctor. You've always been very good to me, over me arthuritis and that trouble with the old waterworks.'

'No bother Lizzie,' said Peter Mayes. 'You come and see me any time.' He spoke very loudly, knowing how deaf Lizzie was, and that she was quite unable to cope with the hearing-aid he had got for her. 'What is it this time?'

'Nothing much doctor. I didn't want to bother you, but me

friend was worried over me wind. Something chronic it is. More like a tornado.'

What the old girl has really got is verbal diarrhoea, thought Peter Mayes. And I don't know of any cure for that. He turned and asked Sister to make up a mixture, as Lizzie continued to rattle on.

'Gets me right here, and the pains go up to me shoulder. Can't get on with me sewing or crochet. There's just no way to sit comfortable.'

'Yes,' said Peter Mayes, taking the glass from Sister. 'Indigestion can be very painful. You drink this up; it will ease things for you.'

Lizzie looked at the glass dubiously. 'Drink it up Lizzie,' the doctor shouted.

She took it, prepared for a nasty taste. To her surprise it was rather pleasant.

'That's quite tasty. Not like the last stuff you give me!' She almost smacked her lips as she handed back the empty glass.

'Glad you like it. We'll have some made up for you, and you must take it after meals.'

'It won't do any good. Nothing does. Gobble me food you see, always have. Can you give me a hand up Sister? Thank you dear. Wind, just wind. Like the poor, always with us.'

The doctor walked with her to the door. Lizzie was still chattering away. 'What with the wind and the waterworks and the arthuritis, life's a misery sometimes. Still, keep your pecker up, eh?'

'That's it Lizzie.' Peter Mayes smiled at her. 'I'll have a bottle of that mixture sent up for you, and you take half a glass every meal. Miss Berryman or Mrs Spencer will see that you do.'

'Thanks doctor, but it won't do any good you know.'

Dr Mayes handed her over to Pat Berryman and went back into his surgery.

'She won't wear the hearing aid we got her, and I don't suppose she'd remember the medicine if an officer didn't take it to her. She's a nice old thing though.'

'That girl's a little beauty, isn't she?' said Sister. And Peter Mayes agreed that she was.

When he went along to Radley's office later that afternoon – he wanted his signature on a transfer form (an unfortunate inmate being sent to a mental hospital) – he asked the Deputy what Jill was in for. Radley asked for her surname and then looked her up in his file.

'Ah yes,' he said. 'I remember now. A very young innocent looking girl, seems to be about sixteen. In fact she's a good bit older. She was a model for teenage clothes – I expect you noticed how small she is – and during one of her modelling sessions she was noticed by a singularly unpleasant type who specialised in pornographic photographs.'

Peter Mayes looked puzzled.

'She's got a simplicity, an innocence, that doesn't fit in with all that.'

Radley glanced at the report he was holding. 'Be your age Peter. Though if it's anything to go by, the psychos say that she is definitely retarded. Anyhow why did she come to see you? VD?'

'Far from it. She's got a strange rash. I hope it's easily explained but I've a feeling it may be psychosomatic.'

When Jill was taken to see the doctor two days later, he was sorry to see that, while the rash was no worse, it was certainly no better, and was starting to spread. He decided to put her on antibiotics, and had the hands dressed again, using a more powerful ointment.

At Association that evening Jill came in for a good deal of needling from the other women. Peter Mayes was the most popular of the doctors at Stone Park and they were rather jealous of what they regarded as his attentions to Jill. Thelma, a sharp, unkind but rather amusing woman, was saying: 'So he's given you a special ointment, has he?'

'Yes,' said Reba when Jill didn't answer. 'Doctor says her skin's ever so delicate.'

'Delicate!' And Thelma muttered an obscene remark to Vi who was sitting next to her, which caused Vi to choke with laughter. Vi was the immensely fat woman who was also a hypochondriac. Hardly a week passed without her applying to see the doctor; she had even managed to spend a week in hospital, having deliberately hurt her arm.

'Bloody poof,' she now said.

'Oh I don't reckon so,' said Thelma. 'I reckon he fancies her. Does the nice doctor fancy you, poppet?'

Jill looked at her with dislike, but she didn't answer. Vi however was only too ready to answer. 'That's it, fancies her just because she's pretty. That ponce would do anything for a pretty bird. You got to be a model girl to get any consideration in this place.'

'Well,' said Thelma, 'you could do some modelling Vi. You could model support stockings for elephants.'

There was a roar of laughter from the women as Vi, glaring at Thelma, heaved herself to her feet and waddled across to her cell. Thelma, delighted with her wit, winked at Jill, but got no reaction.

Old Lizzie who had been sitting in an armchair got up and started towards her cell.

'Tea will be coming up soon Lizzie,' said Pat Berryman, giving her a helping hand. The old lady seemed even more arthritic that afternoon, and her breathing was bad.

'I don't want none, miss. Me indigestion. I'd best have some of me mixture.'

'All right, Lizzie. Once you're back in your cell, I'll get the bottle.'

'Thanks, miss. I'll have a bit of a rest, then I'll be all right supper time.'

Lizzie lay on her bed, and, soon after, the officer brought her her medicine.

'Have a little sleep, Lizzie,' she said. 'That'll make you feel better.'

'Thanks, miss,' said the old woman gratefully. 'You are ever so good to me. I'll get on with my crochet till I doze off.'

On the Wing the women talked and argued and chatted to each other and to the screws. Mrs Weekes had a quiet chat with Jill, whom she rather liked. She didn't properly know what the girl was in for, which was just as well, for if she had she would have been horrified.

Half an hour later tea came up and the women queued for it, talking as they did so.

'Look at that, the Rock of Gibraltar,' said Thelma as she was given a large bun.

'Just what you need. Put hairs on your chest,' replied Mrs Spencer briskly.

'Thanks ever so,' said Thelma ironically and passed on.

Reba was next and then Jill and Mrs Weekes. Mrs Weekes had got hold of a tray knowing that Jill, with her heavily bandaged hands, would have difficulty in carrying her mug of tea.

'Let me have it dearie,' she said. 'That's why I brought the tray.' She noticed the large plate of freshly cooked buns. 'Ooh, don't they look good. Want one?' Jill nodded. Thelma was watching all this.

'Wish I had a lady's maid, like some people seem to have. Nice being waited on, innit Jill?'

'Don't you pay no attention to her,' said Mrs Weekes. She looked round. 'Where's Lizzie?' she asked.

'Got her heartburn,' answered Reba.

'Oh,' said Mrs Weekes. 'She'll be sorry to miss them lovely buns. She likes currant buns. I'll see if I can fetch her one.'

Despite Thelma's jeers she went across to Lizzie's cell, to see if she could do anything for her old friend. But she was too late.

Lizzie lay on the bed, on her special quilt. Her eyes were open and one of her arms trailed over the side of the bed. The other was grasping her chest. On the floor lay a square of crochet with its hook still in it. Mrs Weekes stood staring. Then a look of great sadness came into her face. She knew death when she saw it.

CHAPTER THIRTEEN

As soon as Faye heard the news about old Lizzie, she went up and visited a rather subdued North Wing, for a death on a Wing is not only rare, it is upsetting for the inmates. Janet Harker had stayed on late, of her own accord. The Governor had a word with her and then went to old Lizzie's cell. All her belongings were still there, and Faye felt her personality had not yet left the room. The unfinished piece of crochet lay on the table. What a pity, thought Faye, that this was all going to be taken down, even thrown away. It had taken Lizzie, an old rogue if ever there was one, to make a prison cell into a home. A sudden idea struck Faye and she went out. She looked at the names on the doors and found Mrs Weekes' cell. She went in: the old woman was weeping quietly. She rose when the Governor came in.

'Sit down,' said Faye gently. 'I expect this has been a shock to you, Mrs Weekes.'

'Yes'm. I didn't know she was ill, not proper ill that is.'

'Nor did any of us.'

'At least she went quiet, without suffering,' said Mrs Weekes.

'Yes indeed. Now, I have had an idea. You know Lizzie had no relations in England. Except for that nephew in Australia she was quite alone in the world.'

'And he hadn't written for years, she told me.'

'Exactly,' said Faye. 'So I would like you to have her things.'

Mrs Weekes was so astonished that she stopped weeping. 'Oh no m'm, it wouldn't be right.'

'If you don't have them, they'll be scattered, they might

even be thrown out. You were one of her oldest friends, I know she would like you to take care of them for her.'

'Oh m'm. . . .' Mrs Weekes was quite overcome. 'Thank you.'

'Perhaps you would like to go to the funeral? I expect some of the staff will be going.'

'Oh that would be lovely.' Mrs Weekes dearly liked a nice funeral. 'When will it be?'

'On Monday, I think. Mrs Spencer will tell you.'

Faye rose. A very young looking girl, her hands bandaged, came to the door. She carried a rag doll.

'Is this Jill?' asked the Governor.

Jill nodded shyly.

'Lizzie made her the doll,' said Mrs Weekes. 'Clever with her hands, Lizzie. She used to say, that's what got her in here so often.' She gave a rather shaky grin.

Faye smiled at them both. 'How are your hands, Jill?' she asked.

'OK,' said Jill in what was hardly more than a whisper.

'She's almost retarded,' thought Faye, and she nodded to them and left.

Jill sat holding her doll awkwardly.

'She was going to sew a new dress for her,' she whispered.

'Never mind dearie,' said Mrs Weekes. 'How are the hands?'

Mrs Weekes looked at the girl's arms and saw that the angry blotches had spread outside the bandaged area.

'What did doctor say?' she asked.

'Just said I'd have to have some more ointment. You promised he'd look after me.'

'He will,' said Mrs Weekes. 'He's got to,' and she made up her mind to speak to Mrs Spencer again.

The Governor went and told Miss Harker that she wanted Mrs Weekes to go into Lizzie's cell, permanently, after the funeral, and that nothing was to be moved out of the cell. She also suggested that 'Lock Up' should be delayed for an hour that evening, till nine o'clock, to give the women the benefit of some extra television, after the shock of old Lizzie's death.

'Very well Madam,' said Janet.

And Faye went back to her office.

There had, of course, to be an inquest on Lizzie, and it was arranged for the following afternoon, after the post mortem in the morning. Charles Radley, who went to the inquest, came in and reported to Faye.

She then went up to the Hospital Wing and waited, in his office, for Peter Mayes. When he came in after a short while, she was shocked at his appearance, he looked so drawn and tense.

He came in without saying anything, only giving his head a slight shake as he sat down on the chair behind his desk.

'Was it a heart attack?' asked Faye.

'Angina. She must have had a dozen small attacks before this one. She did often complain of pain.'

'I expect she thought it was her heartburn,' said Faye.

'Yes. She was always beefing on about it. And I, who should have known better, I accepted her own diagnosis. Can you imagine such appalling negligence?'

'No one was blaming you or doubting your ability Peter. The inquest was only a formality.'

'You miss my point. It's I who am blaming myself. Why, she was in here only a day or two ago. I realise now that she was saying something about a pain in her arm – always a classic symptom of angina – but because she was always rabbiting on, I didn't really listen. And as a result old Lizzie is dead.' His voice was very bitter.

'Peter, what are you doing this evening?' Faye asked.

'I had thought of going off to some pub, to think things out while drinking myself silly.'

'That would not be a good idea. Come round to us and have supper and we'll both of us talk to Bill. He's a very sound person.'

'Why should I bother you with my troubles?'

'I bothered you with mine the night that Bill was hijacked,' said Faye with a smile. 'He's got plenty of drink, if that's how you feel.'

Peter Mayes was tempted. He was a lonely man who had reached a crisis in his life. It might be good to talk it over with two friends.

'I'd like that,' he said. 'Could I come round about eight?'

'That would be fine. Don't let me down Peter. We would truly love to see you.'

She leant forward and patted his hand. Then she left.

The doctor sat in his chair trying to fight off his feeling of guilt and depression. One of the young doctors, a bouncy young man with startling red hair (who had already decided that he had no intention of remaining in the prison service since he disliked it), came breezing in, gave Mayes a short lecture on acupuncture, and breezed out again.

Soon after that Sister Baxter came in.

'I had a call from Mrs Spencer on North Wing. She wanted to talk to you, but Mrs Boswell was with you. It's the girl Jill; the rash is spreading. What do you think, doctor?'

Mayes restrained a strong desire to answer, 'What I think is of very little importance as I have proved myself useless at my job and I am going to resign.' Instead he said: 'We'd better get her over and I'll have another look at it. I am puzzled over that one, Sister.'

'So am I,' answered Sister. 'Those swabs you took were completely negative. And yet it's spreading.'

'Perhaps we'd better admit her. Have her brought in tomorrow.'

'Yes sir.' Sister turned to go. At the door she said to

Mayes: 'It's sad about old Lizzie; we shall all miss her. But you mustn't blame yourself, Doctor.'

'Thank you, Sister,' said Mayes: and added, to himself, 'But I must.'

When Faye got home, Bill had beaten her to it. He was sitting in front of the fire, reading the evening paper, and listening, inevitably, to one of the Brandenburgs.

As Faye came into the room he grinned at her.

'Hello, darling,' he said. 'Would you like to go round to the Duncans after supper? They rang up just now.'

Faye shook her head.

'Good,' said Bill. 'I'd rather have an evening to ourselves too.'

'Oh dear,' thought Faye. 'I hope he won't mind about Peter.' Aloud she said:

'I've asked Peter Mayes to supper. He's in a bad way. He was going off to a pub by himself and I thought that was the very last thing. . . .'

'The very last,' agreed Bill. And asked his wife what was wrong.

She explained that Mayes was thinking of leaving. When she had finished he said:

'Would you want him to resign?'

'I would simply hate it. He's dead tired and needs a proper holiday: but he's so good with the women and most of them like him. The new young doctors who come to us are different. None of them seem to have any sense of vocation, and, although they are well trained, they treat the women like case-histories rather than human beings.'

'It must be a pretty boring sort of job for a doctor. One that doesn't stretch him at all.'

'It is. But that isn't the reason why Peter is talking about resigning. Our oldest inhabitant died yesterday and he is blaming himself for her death.'

'Why on earth?'

Faye put him into the picture and then went into the kitchen section to concoct a suitable supper for Peter. He loved good food but did not often, she suspected, get it. He lived in a small flat at the top of a retired doctor's house, and either did for himself or ate with his landlord. In either case the result was dull. She decided to give him coq-au-vin and a cheese soufflé.

She was using the electric mixer and over its busy buzz did not hear the doorbell when it rang. But she heard Bill's voice welcoming Peter Mayes and then Peter's voice saying: 'I came, as I promised Faye, but I don't think I can stay.'

'Why not?' asked Bill.

'I've got a decision to make.'

It sounded, thought Faye, as though Peter's depression was deeper than ever.

'You need a drink,' said Bill. 'What's your tipple?'

'Scotch, if you have it,' said Mayes, and was given one.

'What's this decision?' asked Bill.

'Whether to resign or not.'

'That is a big one.'

Faye came into the room. She thought Mayes looked very tense.

'I've got a delicious supper for you and if you don't stay and eat it I shall be deeply offended,' she said. 'It won't be ready yet, so we can have a long talk.'

'I shouldn't stay,' said Mayes, but his drink had already relaxed him. He slumped down into a chair.

'Yes you should,' said Bill and topped up his glass. 'What I don't understand is, you're a doctor. You must have seen death many times.'

'Of course I have.'

'Then why has this old lady's hit you so hard?'

'Because I should have examined her properly. The post mortem said her condition was long standing.'

'If you had discovered it, how much longer would she had lived?' asked Bill.

'Perhaps a few months. Perhaps not. That isn't the point. I should have seen something. Many diseases have disguised symptoms. They masquerade as other things, heartburn, a pain in the arm. At one time I'd have followed them up.'

'I think you're blaming yourself unnecessarily,' said Bill. 'I remember, about ten years ago, I had to examine a radio mast in Norway. Huge thing. Old for a mast. I had a few girders changed and strengthened the base supports. Two days later it fell to pieces in a storm. Metal fatigue.'

There was a moment's pause, then Mayes said:

'Yes, yes. I get your point. But this was a death.'

'So was that. And I couldn't have prevented it, any more than you could have prevented that old woman's.'

'The truth is, I've stopped looking,' said Mayes. 'So many minor ailments, so many imaginary diseases – I've grown careless.' He sounded utterly depressed and Faye felt it was time for her to intervene.

'Peter, you've grown tired. You run your own surgery and the psychotherapy groups; you head the Drug Unit, and hold minor clinics that ought to be left to the young doctors. You must learn to delegate. If you gave up now it would be a terrible waste.'

'You know,' said Bill, 'Faye and I were talking the other day about you all becoming "institutionalised". But I think that's a necessary part of experience in this day and age. It's only when you've fully accepted the possibilities and limitations of the job that you really know and understand it.'

There was another pause and then Mayes actually smiled.

'You're both right. I must prescribe myself a holiday and a kick in the pants. Could I have another drink?'

As Bill poured it, Faye looked at him with gratitude.

'I could sleep for a week,' said Mayes.

'Just what you need,' said Faye. 'But first come and have supper. It's ready.'

After the meal, which was a success, Bill drove Mayes back to his digs. Faye, greatly relieved, cleared away. 'I believe that Peter has recovered his equilibrium,' she thought thankfully as she coped with the debris of supper.

Several hours before this, on the North Wing, a group of women stood in a huddle, talking in a conspiratorial way.

Thelma was the main spokesman.

'Never even looked at 'er,' she was saying, 'and all he did was give her a glass of medicine.'

'The same could happen to any of us,' said Reba, and Vi added, 'the lot of us could die for all the medical attention we get.'

Mrs Weekes came out of her cell.

'Hey, Georgie,' called Thelma. 'How's the poppet?' For the Wing now treated Jill as though she was a baby or a doll.

Mrs Weekes looked worried. 'That rash is spreading right up her arms. All red and painful.'

'Someone should tell the screws,' said a cross-looking middle-aged woman with a hair lip.

'I did. I talked to Mrs Spencer last night and again this morning.'

'You see? Even when it's reported, nothing's done,' said Thelma indignantly.

They looked round at the sound of the gate being unlocked by Mrs Spencer, to let Sister Baxter through.

'Come to see how the other half lives Sister?' said Mrs Spencer.

'Only to collect a customer. Not staying, I'm afraid,' answered Sister smiling. 'Is Miss Harker in her office?'

'Yes.'

Janet was working at her desk. The women were up to

something, and she didn't know what it was. Pat Berryman was lounging against the wall smoking. There was a knock on the door and she instantly straightened and held the cigarette behind her back. Sister, who had a keen nose, smiled. 'It's only me, Miss Harker.'

Pat Berryman relaxed.

'I've come to fetch Jill Fryer to the Hospital Wing.' And Sister handed Janet the signed transfer order.

'High time too,' muttered Pat Berryman to herself.

'She's not responding to treatment. Dr Mayes wants her in for observation.'

'I'll take you to her cell,' said Janet, and the two women went across the Wing.

'They've come for her,' said Mrs Weekes.

'Just as well,' said Vi and Thelma added. 'See? It takes a death to stir things up.'

Mrs Weekes hurried after the Assistant Governor and the Sister.

'Oh please, Miss. Can Jill take her doll? She do love it.' And she added in a lower voice. 'She's like a little kid in some ways.'

Miss Harker looked a question at Sister Baxter.

'Well, it's not really allowed. But as she's going to be on her own, let her take it, and we'll see what doctor says.'

Jill was led away, not without difficulty for the women were crowding round her.

'Out of the way,' said Mrs Spencer. 'Let Sister get through the gates.'

Jill went, holding Sister's hand, trustingly, like a little girl. They all watched her go and then turned to each other again.

'Did you hear that?' asked Thelma. 'She's going to be in one of them wards all on her own.'

'Poor little kid,' said Mrs Weekes.

'It's because she's infectious,' said Reba. 'And now we could all come down with it. They left it too late.'

'Like Lizzie,' added another woman.

'Yeah. They let *'er* die. Soon it could be all of us.'

Janet had been listening to this. She would have to do something. But they were becoming so worked up that if she broke them up, it might start a riot. Conscious of her own shortcomings, she put out a call for Mrs Armitage, who arrived quite soon, as she had only been on the Centre. She looked at the bunch of women, muttering among themselves.

The Chief went into the office and she, Janet and the officers spoke quietly.

'It's a bit like this all over the prison,' said Mrs Armitage. 'But of course it's worse on this Wing.'

'They're working themselves up,' said Janet. 'Somehow we must stop it.'

'If I could have a word with them, Miss Harker?' said Mrs Armitage.

Janet felt a great sense of relief. However disagreeable the Chief might be, she was a tower of strength in a situation like this.

'Yes Chief,' she answered. 'But I warn you, they are in a funny mood.'

'Have you a small notebook I could borrow?' the Chief asked her, which seemed to Janet something of a *non sequitur*.

'Yes,' she answered, giving her one. 'But why—?' But Mrs Armitage was already moving towards the women, who were by now thoroughly worked up.

'They let Lizzie die.'

'They shouldn't be allowed to get away with it.'

'They can't just hush it up and forget it.'

'We got a right to proper treatment.'

'And the poppet's infectious. So what about us?'

Suddenly Mrs Armitage was among them.

'A word with you, ladies,' she said in her most authoritative way.

The women were so surprised that they turned to listen. The muttering stopped.

'I know you were all upset by Lizzie's death.'

Thelma opened her mouth to say something, then thought better of it.

'She was a great character, Lizzie. Very popular. Of course she was an old woman. And with her heart condition, we were lucky to have had her for so long.'

'What heart condition?' asked Reba, and another woman added. 'It was so sudden.'

'That's the way it goes with heart trouble. Sharp and sudden. The Coroner said at the Inquest today she'd been living on borrowed time for years.'

There was a stunned silence.

Mrs Armitage continued.

'There is one other thing that may have been worrying you. Jill Fryer. She is not, I'm afraid, very well. But Sister Baxter particularly wanted you to know that Dr Mayes took swabs from her several days ago. She is not in any way infectious and you none of you have anything to fear.'

There was silence from the women. Most of them looked relieved: a few were disappointed. It was something to do, getting things stirred up.

When Mrs Armitage spoke again, there was a subtle change in her voice.

'As you may have heard, Lizzie's funeral is the day after tomorrow. Madam will be going; so will I, and as many of the staff as can be spared. Now, it will only be a quiet affair, but knowing how fond you all were of Lizzie and so worried too, I am sure you would like to contribute a few pence each to buy her some flowers from this Wing. South Wing has already made a collection and I'm sure you wouldn't want to do less. Just a few pence from each of you. No compulsion of course, only what you can spare, seeing you were so upset about her death. So, Mrs Weekes, would you like to write down the names of those who wish to contribute.'

'Yes'm,' said Mrs Weekes, who had already privately determined in her own mind to put down two weeks wages. She moved among the women whose mood had rapidly changed. Even Thelma had quietened down and they were arguing among themselves as to how much or how little they would contribute; and what kind of flowers they would get old Lizzie; and what would they write on the card? Mrs Armitage went across to Miss Harker who was standing with Mrs Spencer, wrapped in admiration.

'I don't think you will have any more bother with them now,' she said.

'Thank you,' said Janet. 'We are truly grateful,' and she thought to herself as Mrs Armitage left, how ironic it was that this woman, so cold and unsympathetic in some ways, could yet control a difficult and excited group of women with such skill.

Jill lay in the small hospital cubicle. Sister Baxter had given her new dressings on her hands and up her arms. When she helped her undress, Sister had noticed that her thighs were now covered with small marks, red and angry, yet she had no temperature and her pulse was normal. Sister was puzzled. She would have a talk with Dr Mayes tomorrow.

She gave Jill a hot drink, which the girl drank obediently.

'This will make you sleep,' said Sister. 'Good night, dear. Doctor Mayes will see you in the morning.'

Jill lay staring into the half dark, awkwardly clutching the rag doll that Lizzie had made for her. So she was here at last. In hospital, where the doctor was. What she had always wanted. Perhaps he'd look in and see her soon. She put her thumb in her mouth and sucked it, day dreaming. And then, because the sedative which Sister had given her in her hot drink had been a strong one, she slept.

CHAPTER FOURTEEN

It was a fine day for old Lizzie's funeral. In the cemetery a cherry tree was in full blossom and a thrush shouted its heart out, almost drowning the mutter of the impersonal clergyman as he hurried through the service. Still, thought Faye, the old woman had a very respectable show of flowers. She would have liked that; and yesterday in chapel the attendance had been treble what it usually was, as word had gone round that the Chaplain was going to say a few words about Lizzie. There was no doubt about her popularity.

Faye glanced round. Mrs Armitage, Miss Parrish, Mrs Spencer and Miss Dudgeon. And of course Mrs Weekes, smart in her best black, and very conscious of her position of trust in being there.

Barely audible the voice of the priest droned on. . . . 'In the midst of life we are in death. Of whom may we seek for succour, but of thee, O Lord, who for our sins art justly displeased. . . .'

Old Lizzie's crimes, Faye thought: Would they be classed as sins?

The coffin was lowered, and two men in overalls carrying spades stepped forward. Mrs Weekes looked a question at Faye who gave a tiny nod. Mrs Weekes stepped forward and threw a bunch of violets, which she was carrying, into the grave. With the thud of earth on the grave, the service was over. Faye turned and, after a word of thanks to the priest, walked to the big black car which stood waiting.

'Can we all pile in?' said Faye.

'Mrs Weekes and I can walk Madam,' said Mrs Spencer. 'It's only a short way and I expect old Georgie would like a bit of an outing.'

So the two women set out together. When they reached the prison and got back to North Wing, Mrs Weekes was made much of, for most of the inmates wanted to know what the flowers were like.

'They were lovely. Madam's were best and after that, ours.'

After Mrs Weekes had had a cup of tea, Janet Harker called her into the office.

'I expect you'd like to take possession of Lizzie's cell now? I'll come and unlock it for you and then you can clear your belongings out of your old cell.'

Ten minutes later, Georgie Weekes was alone in her new room. You couldn't call it a cell, she thought. It all looked almost too good to touch. The teapot and the cups had been set up on the table. Someone had put a small bunch of flowers on the shelf. Mrs Weekes sat on the bed and stroked the patchwork quilt. 'Took her four years to make that,' she thought. 'I won't let no-one sit on it, either, except the Governor of course.' And she added in a low voice. 'I'll take care of it all for you, Lizzie, honest I will.'

In the Governor's office Faye and her senior Assistant Governor and the Chief were having coffee.

'I'm glad you both came,' said Faye.

'A lot more would have come, if they'd been able to,' said Miss Parrish. 'She was an old rogue of course but you couldn't help liking her.'

'I often wondered if any of those stories of hers were true,' said Mrs Armitage.

'I checked up on a couple of them once,' answered Faye. 'The details were true, she'd just embroidered them a bit.'

'She must have been quite a girl forty years ago,' said Miss Parrish with one of her rare smiles.

The door opened and Charles Radley and Peter Mayes

came in. Faye was glad to see that, although the latter still looked tired, he was no longer in the least tense.

'How was the funeral?' asked Radley.

'Very simple, rather touching. Of course it's not so sad when it's someone as old as Lizzie.'

'Yes, you can accept it more easily then,' said Martha Parrish.

'It's natural,' added Mrs Armitage.

'Coffee?' said Faye, and both men took some from the percolater on a side table.

'Peter has been arranging his holiday,' said Radley. 'I went to Cooks with him. It made me feel quite envious.'

'Where are you going, doctor?' asked Miss Parrish.

'Greece,' said Mayes. 'Cruising on a small boat round the Islands. I'll be away for three weeks.'

'And come back a new man,' added Radley.

'I hope so.'

'Lucky creature,' said Faye. 'When d'you go?'

'In about a fortnight, if that's OK by you. I want to get everything shipshape here and to brief young Russell. I must try and get Jill Fryer's case finalised too. I've had her transferred to Hospital, Faye.'

'She'll enjoy that,' said Mrs Armitage with a bite in her voice.

'What d'you mean Chief?' asked Mayes.

'She loves people running round after her. Half the women on the Wing mother her. She had old Georgie Weekes acting like a lady's maid.'

'She's like a child. And most children respond to kindness,' said Mayes.

'And most children are very cunning too.' The bite in the Chief's voice was more pronounced than before. 'If you ask me this is what she's been working for, being sent to Hospital. Sister makes a fool of her in my opinion.'

'I'm sorry, Chief, but I don't want your opinion in this

matter. My opinion is that she should be in for observation, and what I say goes.'

'Hey!' said Radley. 'End of first round.'

Miss Parrish rose tactfully and so did Mrs Armitage but with a bad grace.

'We must get back now,' said the former. 'Thank you for the cup of coffee, Madam. You coming, Mollie?'

'Yes,' said Mrs Armitage. 'I certainly am,' and she strode out of the room.

As the door shut Radley said: 'What was all that in aid of?'

'The girl has a rash which Peter thinks is not infectious.'

'I know it isn't. I've had swabs analysed. But it's getting worse. It was an allergy to start with, but it should have cleared up by now. I don't understand the Chief's attitude.'

'She thinks the girl is an arch manipulator.'

'Which is nonsense,' said Mayes, who had, oddly enough, been completely deceived by Jill's gentle ways and guileless looks.

'Is it?' said Faye, who had not. 'I know she's very child-like but, as the Chief says, children can be horribly cunning.'

'Wait a minute!' said Radley. 'Is this the girl with the face of an angel who was involved in a porno photographic session?'

'Yes.'

'Did you say "childlike"?' asked Radley with a sour smile.

'I did,' said Mayes.

'I don't suppose you saw the photographs that she was convicted on? I did. Whew!'

After the two men had left Faye, as they walked to their various offices, Mayes said:—

'Those photographs. Were they straight porn?'

'What d'you mean by that?'

'A twosome.'

'Far from it,' said Radley. 'This was very curious stuff indeed. If I remember rightly, some of the pictures involved a chimp. And that pure little face with its innocent smile, mixed up with that lot. Very titillating. I can quite see that Jill must be a valuable property to her employers.'

Which set the doctor thinking; and when he got back to the Hospital Wing he sent for Sister.

'I have been thinking about Jill,' he said. 'I want to make quite sure that rash isn't self-inflicted.'

'But doctor, the path lab said—'

'Not the original rash, but this new one. Anyhow, to satisfy myself this is what I propose to do. . . .' and he told Sister his plan.

On her bed in the narrow cubicle Jill lay, helpless. Her hands were tightly bandaged and padded with cotton wool. Huge, shapeless, heavy, they lay useless at her side. She twisted and turned, hating the doctor and the nurse who had brought her to this. She was completely helpless and had to be fed by Sister.

'How long?' she had asked Sister in her whisper, and Sister had answered, 'only for four or five days dear,' and continued to spoon feed her. Jill had looked down, away from Sister's kind eyes, to hide the hate in her own. Four or five days meant very little to Jill. She was, as Faye had said, like a child who lived from day to day. Now was forever, and now was lying here bandaged and helpless. Like a child; but like a very evil child, who found the unnatural life she had been leading before she was convicted not only bearable but pleasurable.

The Welfare Officer, who had looked after her case before she was sentenced, had been deeply affected by the childish innocence that shone, like a radiance, round her, and had thought she would at the worst get a suspended sentence. Unfortunately for Jill the ancient judge who tried her was also very cynical. He had read the report of her headmaster and had looked at the photographs. Then he had sentenced her to nine months. When she came in to Stone Park, Faye had wondered whether it was really fair to the tax payer to bring in a girl like this, since it was obvious that prison could not cure or even help her. Though perhaps the new method with its plethora of trained psychiatrists might be able to do something for her. But would it?

Sister came back to see Jill before she went off duty that evening.

'All right little love?' she asked, looking at the innocent flower-like face on the pillow.

Jill nodded. She was humming to herself and thinking about that nice place, Amster somewhere, where Tony was going to take her to live when she got out of this bleeding hole. 'Much less fuss there,' he'd said to her. 'Plenty of games to play.' Children's games, thought Jill and giggled inwardly.

'Bless her,' thought Sister. 'She's singing herself nursery rhymes.'

Jill was indeed singing a song to the tune of 'Nuts in May,' and it was as well that Sister couldn't hear the words, for they were utterly obscene.

Sister left, and Jill, unable to suck her thumb, turned and bit savagely into her pillow.

The day before Peter Mayes left for his holiday he had a long talk with Faye when he took her out to lunch. He gave her a full briefing on the patients at present in the hospital, and ended by saying:

'Do you know that enormous woman Violet from North Wing?'

'Yes. Mrs Armitage says she is one of the worst skivers.'

'She is indeed. Not a week goes by that she doesn't put in to see me. But this time she's rather overdone it; she's managed to fall off her bed.'

'By mistake or purpose?'

'I wouldn't mind betting on it. She hurt her ankle quite badly, a Potts fracture, not surprising with her weight. She's in plaster, of course, and I imagine she'll be in hospital for two weeks at least. I hope she won't cause too much alarm and despondency.'

'Don't worry, Peter,' said Faye. 'I'll keep an eye. . . . What about Jill Fryer?'

'Thanks to you and the Chief I've managed to clear that one up.'

'Thanks to us?'

'I realised I was treating the symptoms and not the patient. As soon as we immobilized her hands, the rash stopped spreading.'

'So she *had* been doing it herself?'

'Not at first. The original rash was genuine: but when she found the attention it brought her, and how it took her off kitchen work which she loathed, she helped it along, scratching and even biting herself.'

'Not minding the pain?'

'It's a symptom of her particular condition that the pain threshold is very high. I got young Ford to see her.'

Faye was glad to hear that Peter was co-operating with James Ford the newly arrived young doctor whom the Home Office had just appointed.

'I would feel inclined to trust that young man,' she said.

'He knows his stuff,' said Peter Mayes. 'And he's prepared to admit that people have minds as well as bodies, which helps. I've asked him to see if he can impress on Vi the importance of keeping out of hospital in future. She is such hell for the other patients.'

'I know. A tiresome woman. These skivers are a pain in the neck.'

'One can't entirely blame them,' said Mayes. 'It's a game to play; and anything is better than the boredom of prison.'

'I've done what I can,' said Faye. 'But it isn't nearly enough.' She sounded rather despondent. 'You've done an enormous amount,' said Mayes, 'and you know it.'

'So Jill is going back to North Wing?'

'For the moment, with special psychiatric treatment. Of course most of the women will welcome her with open arms; she's a bonus, something to cuddle. If she gets up to her tricks, she'll have to go to a special hospital. I'll leave it to Ford: he's very sound on that side of things.'

'Good,' said Faye.

Two years ago Faye would have agonised over Jill. Now she accepted her as one of the many disturbed women in her care, a shameless and immodest creature who happened by a freak of nature to look like a Botticelli cherub. Aloud she only said, 'Good, Peter, I can see that you are at last beginning to delegate.'

'I've got to, haven't I? Since you more or less ordered me away for this holiday. . . . Imagine it, this time tomorrow, I shall be in Athens.' And he grinned like a schoolboy.

'Are you going straight to the boat?'

'Yes. I'll unwind first. A week on the boat, a week in Crete and a week to do my sightseeing at the end.'

Faye looked at him with some affection, remembering how sympathetic and helpful he had been on the night of Bill's hijacking experience. He still looked tired and not entirely his vigorous self, but this holiday would alter all that. She wondered, not for the first time, why he had never married. An unmarried doctor was something of a rarity. Sometime she might ask him but now was not the moment.

She lifted her glass of Soave – they were lunching at an Italian restaurant – and smiled at him.

'To a happy, unwinding holiday,' she said.

CHAPTER FIFTEEN

One bright afternoon, not long after this, Reba Jowett, always very conscious of her position as 'Chapel Redband,' was in the chapel taking the numbers out of the hymn board and attending to the flowers. The door opened and the Governor came in. Reba, who was standing on a chair, started to step down.

'Good day Madam,' she said.

'Hullo, Reba, I was looking for Mr Prentiss.'

'The Chaplain's not been in here this afternoon, Madam.'

'Thank you.' As Faye turned to go she asked; 'You haven't got much longer now, have you?'

'Only two weeks, Madam.'

'Good. Don't miss your tea. You should get back to your Wing.'

'I'll just get rid of these dead flowers and then I'll be along.'

As she left, Faye hoped that Reba would not be back inside again. But she would not have bet on it. Despite her quiet manner, despite the fact that she was undoubtedly a religious woman, Reba was also a basically dishonest one, as far as money was concerned. Although she would not have dreamt of stealing a packet of biscuits or a tin of soup from a shop, she would not have hesitated to steal the money from anyone's wallet or purse.

Once in a crowded shop, a few days before Christmas, she had seen a woman leave her handbag and move away unconscious of what she had done. Reba had instantly swooped and picked it up, and made for the nearest cloakroom, where she took from the wallet inside the notes it was housing, but did not touch any of the other things in the bag, though they were well worth taking. She also took care to replace the wallet itself. Then she went to the Lost Property Office of the shop and handed the bag in. Within ten minutes it was back with its owner, who was delighted, until she later opened the wallet and found that the twenty pounds she had in it had vanished. Had Reba been asked why she had not kept the bag, she would have answered with genuine surprise: 'I couldn't have done that. It would have been *stealing.*'

Faye knew that the psychiatric social workers had done what they could, but she very much doubted whether Reba's particular mania was curable, for she was well over forty years old. The Chaplain, who found her an invaluable helper, and would miss her when she left, was glad that there was never any collection in Chapel: for if there had been and Reba had been near, it would have led to complications.

The door now opened and he came in. He was an amiable looking man. His job was not an easy one, for the majority of the women looked upon him as one of 'Them', on the other side of the fence. The Church itself is so much part of the Establishment, which had rejected the prisoner and is punishing her, that he was doubly resented.

When the Chaplain had come to Stone Park he had at first doubted the wisdom of his move and had even discussed with his wife the question of leaving, but after a month or two he had realised the tremendous opportunities for missionary work he had, though he was careful not to bring any kind of pressure on the inmates, who were after all a captive congregation.

His week was a busy one, for he had to see every woman on admission and discharge, to spend several hours each day in visiting any woman who wanted to see him, in her cell or on the Wings. On Sundays he had three or four services to take, even though church services are no longer compulsory and the attendance is sometimes sparse.

As he came in to the Chapel, Reba came out of the door which led to the tiny vestry.

'Why Reba,' he said. 'You're late.'

'I'm just going to tea, Mr Prentiss.'

'You've done the brasses beautifully,' he said.

'Thank you. I'll get along now,' and she added. 'I hope that poor girl is all right?'

'There are so many "poor girls" here Reba. Which one do you mean?'

'That Elaine Reynolds who killed her father.'

'Hardly killed. . . .' The Chaplain stopped. It was not for him to discuss one inmate with another; he nodded dismissal to Reba and she left.

He knew that this particular case was rousing tremendous interest among the women. (He did not know that both on North Wing and on the Long Term Wing a strictly forbidden "book" was being made on whether Elaine Reynolds would be found guilty or not.) Like all euthanasia cases it had become a talking point outside as well as in, although it was now subjudice whilst Elaine was in Remand. She came up for trial the next day. The Chaplain had been to visit her in Remand and had found her an intelligent if rather shy girl. He had got on well with her.

He locked the door of the Chapel, reproaching himself for his own weakness as he did so. Basically a shy man, he would have felt embarrassed if anyone, inmate or officer, had come in and found him alone in the chapel praying. This was perhaps a weakness of the Anglican Church. He could not imagine Father O'Callaghan, his Roman Catholic colleague, feeling self-conscious in this way.

He knelt and prayed.

'O blessed Lord, the Father of all mercies, and the God of all comforts: we beseech thee, look down in pity and compassion upon this, thy afflicted servant. . . .' And then dropping the beautiful archaic wording he asked the God in whom he sincerely believed, to rouse Elaine out of the lethargy into which she had sunk, and to grant her strength and wisdom in her ordeal the next day.

Elaine Reynolds was the daughter of a prosperous solicitor. She was an only child and lived with her parents in an agreeable house near Farnham. She had, since childhood, been devoted to her father. She had done well at school and had wanted to train as a nurse, but her mother was adamant that she should stay at home and "give a hand"; so Elaine was that anachronism, a daughter living at home. After a month or two she was so bored that her father arranged for her to do a short secretarial course and then took her into his office on a part-time basis. This had caused her to become closer than ever to him; for her mother was a busy do-gooder. She was Chairman of the Church Guild, Secretary of the Women's Institute and on countless committees. She was out of her house more often than she was in.

About two years before this, her father had called her into his study one evening. Then, calmly, for he was a brave man, he told her he had an inoperable cancer. For a time he had continued with his work, but soon this became impossible, and he had to hand over to his partner.

Elaine then threw up her own work and proceeded to devote her entire life to him. Her mother was glad not to have a professional nurse in the house, and did not suggest such a thing. She pooh-poohed their doctor when he suggested that Elaine should have some help with the night nursing, saying (quite misleadingly) that she herself could do what was wanted until her husband recovered. She could not face the fact that he would not recover, and neither Elaine nor her father wanted to force her to do so.

For eighteen months Elaine watched her father slowly disintegrate. And one day she realised that life had become unbearable for him. Two things had happened in the same week. The indignity of incontinence had begun, and for him, perhaps an even worse blow, he could no longer do *The Times* crossword puzzle, which he had for years finished within a stipulated time each morning. He used to say that it cleared his mind for the day's work. But, on this particular day, he had dropped his pen and had said, looking at Elaine with despair in his eyes, 'It's no good, I can't use my mind any more. It's those drugs that have done it.'

Elaine had hugged him gently, for he was painfully thin, and had dropped a light kiss on his forehead.

'Don't worry Dad,' she lied to him. 'You're just having an off day.'

That was when she made up her mind.

The next day she had given him a lethal dose of the morphine which had been prescribed to ease his pain. Their doctor was away on holiday and the locum, who had been told that Mr Reynolds would probably live for another two or three months, had insisted on an inquest. As a result Elaine had been arrested and sent to the Magistrates Court, where, instead of being granted bail, she had been committed for trial, and was now in the Remand Wing.

The Governor was discussing her case after a general staff meeting in her office.

'I do feel so sorry for her,' Faye was saying, 'as she was obviously utterly devoted to her father.'

'It is unlikely that she will be found guilty,' said Mayes. 'The general climate of opinion on euthanasia is gradually changing.'

'Yes,' said Faye. 'But I don't understand why as a first offender who had absolutely no record Elaine was not allowed bail.'

'I can tell you that,' said Miss Clarke. 'One of the probation officers told me. It was something her mother said when the police first came to see Elaine. She apparently gave the impression that her husband had longed to go on living and that Elaine was tired of nursing him. From what I've seen of Elaine I don't believe it.'

'I've got tomorrow off, and I've a good mind to look in at the Court,' said Miss Clarke.

'Nothing like a busman's holiday,' said Peter Mayes, cheerfully. Since his holiday in Greece he was in permanently good spirits.

And Charles Radley added: 'My bet is on a suspended sentence, or probation. I know that is what her lawyer expected, I had a word with him last week.'

The following afternoon Mrs Armitage was in the Centre, looking at the books and talking to Janet Harker, when Pat Berryman came past.

'Have you heard, Chief?' she asked.

'Heard what?'

'It came over the radio in the Sewing Shop. Elaine Reynolds has got two years.'

'Two years?' said Janet surprised.

'She's lucky not to get more,' said Mrs Armitage shortly.

'How can you say that?' asked Janet.

'She killed her own father. Poisoned him.'

'For his own sake,' said Pat Berryman.

'That's what she says. In any case it doesn't make it right. Now, if you'll excuse me....'

And she walked angrily away.

'Maybe I shouldn't have mentioned it,' said Pat Berryman.

'I'm glad you did,' said Janet.

All over the prison people were talking about the verdict.

Radley and Peter Mayes discussed it as they converged on the passage leading to the Governor's office.

'I thought she'd get a suspended sentence,' said the doctor.

'I was prepared to bet on it,' answered Radley.

When they got to Faye's office she looked at the men.

'So Elaine got two years,' she said. 'I must say I am surprised. If ever there was a mercy killing this was one. She had absolutely nothing to gain from her father's death.'

'Liz Clarke said she'd go to court,' said Peter Mayes. 'Does anyone know whether she did?'

A knock on the door answered them. Miss Clarke came in. She looked angry.

'Have you heard?' she demanded. 'Two years!'

'I gather you don't approve,' said Faye in her Governor's voice.

'Do you, Governor?'

'Fortunately we're not asked to approve or disapprove, or we would all go mad. Our job is to uphold the judgment of the Courts.'

'But you must have an opinion?'

'I have,' said the Governor.

'What happened in Court, Liz?' asked Radley.

'At first it seemed all right. Elaine must have made a good impression, quiet but audible; sad, of course, but no histrionics. The father's partner gave evidence and it was established that Elaine had nothing to gain from his death: their own doctor, not the locum, said how devotedly she'd nursed her father. And then her mother was called.'

'What happened then?' asked Faye.

'Disaster. She said firmly that her husband had borne his suffering cheerfully and that he was looking forward to recovering and had never wanted to die.'

'Good God,' said Radley.

'How did it effect Elaine?'

'Very badly. She went very white as though she was going to faint. And when she was recalled she seemed to freeze up. She was almost inaudible.'

'That always infuriates a judge,' said Radley.

'Who was it?' asked Faye.

'Old Forbes-Duncan.'

'Bad luck,' said Radley. 'He's a bit deaf at the best of times.'

'If you ask my opinion,' said Miss Clarke, which in fact nobody had, 'after the mother's evidence the jury went right against Elaine.'

'It sounds pretty damning,' said Mayes. 'Did the mother seem a hysterical type?'

'Far from it.'

'Of course they had to find Elaine guilty of manslaughter, but one would have expected a recommendation to mercy.'

'So now she's on our guest list for some time.'

'Yes,' said Faye. 'She must see her lawyer to set an Appeal in motion.'

'Don't let her hope too much,' said Charles Radley. 'After all, legally speaking euthanasia is a crime. And it's the law that counts.'

'Then the sooner the law is changed, the better,' said Miss Clarke: and, silently, Faye agreed with her.

There was a knock on the door and Mrs Armitage came in. Radley seized the opportunity to mutter something about the Works Office, and left.

'You wanted me Madam?' said the Chief.

'Yes. I expect you have heard about Elaine Reynolds?'

'Yes madam,' said Mrs Armitage brusquely.

'I have decided to put her on North Wing.'

'North Wing?' The Chief sounded surprised. 'I thought she'd be in the Special Observation Unit.'

This was a unit kept for any dangerous or violent prisoners.

'Why?' asked Mayes.

'Isn't it obvious doctor?'

'She's not violent,' said Faye.

'She killed her own father,' said the Chief.

'The circumstances that drove her to that are not likely to be repeated,' said the doctor.

'With respect, sir,' said Mrs Armitage. 'You're going by her conduct on Remand. People often change once they're sentenced. There's no longer a pretence to keep up.'

'I don't think that applies to this girl,' said Faye firmly. 'Anyhow we'll ask the Chaplain and Miss Harker for reports after she's been in a week.'

'For what they're worth.'

Faye was taken aback. Mrs Armitage was not usually so rude about her colleagues.

'I trust their judgment. Don't you?'

'We've had this out before, Madam. The Chaplain thinks the best of everyone. Well, I suppose that is his function. But Miss Harker. She's never learnt.'

'Learnt what?' asked Mayes.

'That some prisoners can be dangerous, and need watching carefully.'

'I often agree with you Chief, but not on this,' answered Mayes. 'I don't think Elaine Reynolds needs to be watched.'

'I think she needs sympathy and help,' added Miss Clarke.

Mrs Armitage seemed about to burst.

'She is so angry,' thought Faye, 'that she is in danger of losing her control.'

'Sympathy?' she answered. 'During my years with the Prison Service, I have seen all our attitudes change, to criminals, to their treatment, to punishment. A lot of it I have welcomed but there comes a time when we must stop and take a look, and get our priorities right. I think, just for once, that we should care a little more about the victim and a little less about the criminal.'

Mrs Armitage finished her peroration, for it was no less, with a snap, and stood looking both belligerent and embarrassed at the same time. Her audience regarded her, Faye with surprise, Mayes with amusement and Liz Clarke with anger. After a pause Faye asked: 'Do you know the girl in question?'

'I've seen her in remand, Madam. I've never spoken to her.'

'And you've never seen or heard anything from any officer?'

'Only what I've read.' Her rage had abated and she now sounded somewhat sulky.

Faye spoke seriously. 'Then I believe we are more qualified to judge her. We have all talked to her. She will go to North Wing because I think it best. It will be my responsibility. And I am quite sure there will be no trouble tomorrow.'

Mrs Armitage answered stiffly. 'I only hope you're right Madam, on both counts. And now if you'll excuse me, the new admissions will be here any minute so I'll get along to reception.'

And she was gone, shutting the door with a bang.

Mayes whistled. 'What on earth is that in aid of?'

'I can't imagine. I know she's always disapproved of my ideas, but I can't think what has stirred her up. Do you know, Liz?'

Miss Clarke shrugged. 'She's always been a bit difficult, but in the last weeks I've seen a change. Of course I know she's always been rabidly against euthanasia.' She turned to Faye. 'There was an euthanasia case before you came when Mrs Armitage was very nearly reprimanded by the Governor.'

'Perhaps Miss Parrish will know what's wrong,' said Mayes. 'She's about the only intimate the Chief has got in here.'

'I'll have a word with her,' said Faye.

CHAPTER SIXTEEN

Janet Harker was filling up the names of the two new admissions in her register, Elaine Reynolds and June Mercer. She heard the gates being unlocked and looked up as Miss Dudgeon brought the two women through. Elaine seemed in a state of shock, as many prisoners did on their first day: especially those who, like Elaine, had not expected to be sentenced.

Both prisoners carried small bags with a few personal possessions they had been allowed to keep. June was a brassy young woman, who had left girlhood behind her: she was trendily dressed and sexually agressive; a 'hostess', part-time prostitute, 'model'. She was not in for a long sentence, and, having been in twice before, was not in the least cast down.

'Wait here,' said Officer Dudgeon and went into the office.

A group of women watched Elaine curiously. They had all heard about her case and had seen her photograph on television. One of the women waved to June, who waved back.

'Here we are,' she said to Elaine. 'Home from Home.'

Elaine didn't answer. She was overcome by the noise, the impersonality of her reception, and the feeling of utter finality. Some of the other women came drifting towards them.

'Well! If it ain't June. I thought you was never coming back here?' It was Barbara speaking. She was a handsome, vigorous looking Trinidadian with the magnificent white teeth of her race.

'I tried the straight bit, but I got hard up,' said June.

'How long you get?' asked Barbara.

'Only three months.' June caught sight of Reba. 'Hallo

Reeb,' she said. Then catching sight of the red band on Reba's arm. 'Don't tell me they've made you a trusty?'

'Chapel Redband,' said Reba in a prim voice.

'Chapel?' June grinned. 'I bet you was choked when you found they didn't take no collection.'

Reba bridled at this, and the other women laughed.

'You know who this is, eh?' and June nudged Elaine.

'Yeah. She's been in all the papers.'

'I thought she was going to get off,' said Reba.

'Well you was wrong, wasn't you?' said June.

They were all staring at Elaine who felt exposed, almost as if she were naked. Fortunately Miss Dudgeon came out of the office.

'Break it up. You can talk later. Come along, you two.'

Janet Harker greeted June with, 'I'm suprised to see you back, June.'

'Are you?' said June, to which there was no answer.

'You'll be in Number Twelve with Barbara.'

'Hey! I don't want to be with no chocolate drop. Can't I share with Elaine?'

She glanced at Elaine, who did not look up or speak.

'No,' said Janet. 'Elaine will be in Number Seven.'

'On her tod?'

Janet nodded. June's expression hardened.

'That's nice innit? So you've got friends in high places, eh? You won't need me then.'

'Here you are,' said the Assistant Governor and handed Officer Dudgeon a white card with June's number on it. With a final nudge to Elaine, June went out, followed by the officer.

Elaine stood silently looking at the floor.

'You are to have a cell to yourself,' Janet said. 'To give you time to adjust. Come along and I'll show it to you. The Governor thought you'd rather be by yourself. If you'd rather share, let me know.'

Elaine shook her head.

'Supper's at seven thirty and lock up at eight o'clock. The routine here is a little different from Remand. There's a time table on the wall outside. Have a look at it.'

Elaine nodded slightly and sat on the bed as though her legs would no longer support her. Janet could not help feeling moved by the girl's dumb misery.

'I know it must seem unbearable at the moment. But it will get better. Later the Chaplain is coming to see you. I'll leave you now; I'll look in again before I go off duty.'

Left alone, Elaine looked round the bare cell. Everything seemed to be pressing on her, the trial, her mother's evidence, the destruction of her world. She was still in a state of shock. Later, the Chaplain came in to see her. She couldn't listen to what he was saying. She knew he was trying to be kind, but at the moment she simply could not make the effort needed to answer him. He realised the futility of his visit, and got up to go.

At the door he paused. 'Remember that many people are thinking of you, people you have never met, with great sympathy.'

Elaine gave a half smile and nodded, but did not speak. 'I'm getting nowhere,' thought the Chaplain. 'I'll try again tomorrow.'

Outside the cell Reba asked him how Elaine was.

'We mustn't rush her,' he answered.

'Of course not,' said Reba. 'Poor thing.'

June and Barbara were watching this exchange.

'Hey, Padre,' said June. 'Fancy her, do you?'

'Talking to her, June. Trying to help.'

'She got the blues?' asked Barbara.

'She must 'ave,' said June. 'She thought she'd got away with it.'

'You know I can't discuss it,' said the Chaplain.

'Why not? Why don't you come and discuss it with me,

Padre?' The listening women grinned. 'In my cell. I'd give you a better time than any of them.'

Barbara giggled loudly. June was flaunting herself in front of the Chaplain. Suddenly Mrs Armitage came out of the office.

'Stop that at once, June,' she ordered.

'I was only . . .' began June.

'I know what you were doing. The rest of you if you're not watching that box, switch it off. It's nearly time for classes anyhow.'

June moved quickly to hide behind Barbara. Mrs Armitage was one of the few people she was afraid of. The Chief spoke quietly to Mr Prentiss.

'I'd try to avoid that one, Sir,' she said.

'I think I could handle it.'

'All the same, it's best not to let the situation arise.'

Just then Janet Harker appeared.

'What's been going on?' she asked sensing that a situation was brewing.

'One of the women seemed to resent my visiting Elaine Reynolds,' said the Chaplain.

Before Janet could answer, Mrs Armitage burst out, 'I knew there'd be trouble, putting her on an open Wing.'

'Madam thinks it best for her, and so do I.'

'Of course,' said the Chief sarcastically, 'we mustn't let her think she is being punished. That would never do.'

'I don't think we need worry about that,' said the Chaplain quietly. 'What I'm afraid of is that none of us could punish her as much as she will punish herself.'

Faye rang Martha Parrish on South Wing and asked her to look in on her way home. When she arrived, Faye gave her a glass of sherry and chatted of this and that until she felt ready to come to the point. Then she said in her most diplomatic way:

'I wonder if you can help me? Confidentially. About Mrs Armitage.'

Martha Parrish looked at her steadily.

'In what way can I help?'

'I think you know her better than anyone else here. She is not a woman whom one can approach easily and I am worried over two things. One of them is the fact that she is violently antagonistic to Elaine Reynolds, quite irrationally so.'

'The euthanasia girl? Surely that is easily explained. When Ted – when her husband was first so badly injured by that prisoner, he was in agony for months: and what was worse, they told him that it was unlikely that he would ever move again. When they finally sent him home she was in a terrible state and used to beg and implore Molly to put him out of his misery. She went through a dreadful time that year, but she was adamant. And finally, they did come up with some new drugs which did wonders for him. But those years left their mark on her.'

'Did she tell you this herself?'

'No. Ted Armstrong told me. Have you met him, Mrs Boswell?'

'Yes. He's a nice man. But I felt there was something worrying him and it's reacting on his wife. I don't know whether you've noticed it but she has been reverting to the strict disciplinarian that she was when I first came here.'

'Not a bad thing really. The inmates respect her. But I know you think that both she and I don't treat them softly enough. It's a thing we won't ever agree on.' She smiled as she said it, for she liked the Governor though she did not agree with her liberal ideas.

'The trouble is that she has grown so disagreeable with the rest of the staff, though probably not to you, that I've been wondering whether I'd have a strike of the officers on my hands. Perhaps you could have a word with her?'

'I'll see what I can do. It may be that she is worrying over Ellen.'

'Ellen? . . . The daughter?'

'Yes. I can't tell you the story; that would be betraying a confidence. But it is something she worries over very much indeed.' Martha Parrish rose, dismissing herself. She was a woman of real authority, governor material thought Faye, if only she had not been so reserved.

'Thank you for my nice drink,' she said, and left.

The next morning, as the officers arrived to work they found a group of people gathered round the gates at Stone Park.

They carried banners with slogans like, "Mercy for Mercy Killers," or "Release Reynolds," and they called to the women as they went through, 'What's it feel like to lock *her* up?'

There were heated letters in the newspapers as well as leading articles.

Faye had a staff meeting that morning and naturally the subject came up.

'Surely you all agree,' Faye said, 'that this girl must be helped, even if it means bending the rules a bit.'

Miss Clarke and Janet and the Chaplain agreed warmly, but the Doctor and the Deputy were silent, while Mrs Armitage said:

'We must be careful Madam. The other women resent her, as it is. If we bend the rules for Elaine, it will be seen as overt preferential treatment.'

'Charles?' said Faye.

'I agree with Chief. It's too soon. The case is getting a lot of publicity, so anything that's done for her or to her is bound to get out. In her case there are extenuating circumstances, but euthanasia is still a crime. She's been convicted.

We can't direct the staff to give her preferential treatment. It would be disastrous for her and it could be seen outside as criticism of the law.'

'Peter?' said Faye.

'It's a tricky one,' said the doctor.

'Oh, come on,' said Liz Clarke. 'You agreed what she did couldn't be called a crime.'

'Strictly speaking, perhaps not. But I'm certainly not going to make a pronouncement without knowing the whole medical history.'

'Her father was dying,' said Janet.

'Yes. The point is, he could have lived for another three or four months.'

'Lived?' said Miss Clarke angrily. 'In perpetual agony, only kept going by drugs.'

'In some cases, euthanasia seems to be the only humane solution,' said Peter Mayes, 'but as a doctor I have sworn to maintain life as long as possible. And there is no concrete proof that her father wanted to die.'

'Just the opposite, according to her mother,' said Mrs Armitage.

There was a pause. Faye turned to the Chaplain.

'Mr Prentiss, what do you say?'

'It's a question on which I can see all sides,' he answered in a somewhat evasive way.

'Well, why not tell us simply one of them,' asked Miss Clarke.

'I don't know that I can,' answered the Chaplain. 'Not simply. She was an intelligent, sensitive girl, very close to her father. She suffered with him until it reached a stage that was no longer endurable. But did that give her the right to take another person's life?'

'You tell us,' said the doctor.

'No one has that right. The strongest commandment is,

'Thou Shalt Not Kill.' Mr Prentiss sounded on firmer ground now.

'It's easy for you, isn't it,' said Miss Clarke. 'All you do is hide behind platitudes. You never offer any answers.'

Faye felt it was time to intervene.

'Really Miss Clarke . . .' she began, when the Chaplain interrupted her.

'No, Governor. She's quite correct. Only I don't think my function is to provide pat answers, but to lead people to find their own. And again,' he turned to Miss Clarke, 'the viewpoint of my calling, of my training, is so different from your humanist approach and the structure in which we both have to work, here, that I have to conceal my own thoughts and beliefs behind platitudes, to be able to function at all.'

There was another pause. 'Faye has lost this round, I fear,' thought Charles Radley, while the Governor thought to herself, 'I only hope that cleared the air. But I rather doubt it.'

And she turned to the next item on the agenda.

When Elaine had been on the Wing for about three days, she began to come out of her state of partial shock. She no longer refused her food, and had even glanced at the magazines that Officer Dudgeon brought in to her.

When the Chaplain came in to her cell, she was able to talk to him.

'So many people want to help you,' he was saying, 'not with easy forgiveness, or charity, but with understanding.'

Elaine shook her head. 'No one can understand,' she said. 'I don't know myself now. I was so sure it was right; I could see what I had to do and I was sure he wanted it. But after what my mother said in court, I'm not certain any more.'

'If you could put the clock back, would you do it again?' asked Mr Prentiss.

'Yes,' she said. 'I would. I would do it again. That's why I can't be forgiven, because I'm not sorry.'

'Would you like to pray with me?' asked the Chaplain.

Elaine shook her head. 'No thank you,' she said.

Feeling himself dismissed, the Chaplain went out on to the landing. He saw Reba was reading there. He called to her and led her aside.

'Could you do something to help me? Could you try and talk to Elaine?'

Reba stiffened. 'That's easier said. She thinks she's too good for us. She doesn't talk to us.'

'She's been in shock. She's just coming out of it. I thought you, of all people, would be charitable to her.'

'If you think it would help, Mr Prentiss.'

'She has little in common with anyone here. She needs a friend,' he answered.

'I'll do what I can. But I'm discharged myself in a week's time.'

'Thank you, Reba. Try and get her to come to chapel. It might help her.'

'I'll do all I can,' said Reba, using her holier-than-thou voice.

After supper Reba waited till most of the women were watching television or playing cards, and went across to Elaine's cell. As she crossed the landing, Mrs Weekes came out of her cell.

'That poor girl,' she said. 'Maybe she'd like to come and have tea with me one day?'

'Perhaps,' said Reba. 'When she comes out on Association you must ask her.'

At the door of Elaine's cell she paused.

'I hope you don't mind me looking in. My name's Reba Jowett. The Chaplain said I might call on you.'

'I see,' said Elaine who was still very tense.

Reba came in and sat on the chair.

'I know just how you're feeling. You can't believe what's happened to you. The way everything has stopped. All the things you've taken for granted.'

'Yes,' said Elaine.

Reba continued talking sympathetically, and gradually Elaine started to thaw. She found it a tremendous relief to have someone to talk to who had been through the same sort of experience as she had. When the Governor had come to see her she had been tongue tied. But within a few days she found she was talking more freely to Reba, and could even tell her about the terrible shock it was when her mother had spoken against her in court.

'I'm going out on Tuesday,' said Reba. 'Would you like me to go and see her?'

'Oh, I wish you would.'

'Then I will. Where does she live?'

And Elaine gave her her mother's address.

Reba took it and changed the subject.

'Why don't you come to Chapel? The Chaplain would be pleased. Very few women go. He's such a good man.'

'Yes,' said Elaine. 'I'll come with you tomorrow.'

'Good,' said Reba.

'Where are you going when you're discharged? What will you do outside?'

'The Lord will provide,' said Reba piously, and added, 'I'll pray for you and keep you in my thoughts.'

CHAPTER SEVENTEEN

A few days after Reba left, the Governor went to see Elaine in her cell. She found her to be much less withdrawn, and more ready to talk. She realised that Elaine was worrying deeply over her mother and the totally unexpected evidence she gave.

'I wonder if she is ill,' said Elaine.

Faye suggested that Miss Clarke should look into this, and Elaine was very grateful for the suggestion.

It was encouraging, thought Faye, that, thanks to the efforts of Janet Harker and the other officers (with the exception of Mrs Armitage), Elaine was gradually emerging from her shell. She had been 'to tea' with Georgie Weekes. She had been allotted work, in the sewing shop as she was an excellent needlewoman: she was making some curtains for the Association room, and was also helping Barbara to make a child's dress. She had gone to Chapel on the Sunday and to any midday services which the Chaplain held. After less than a fortnight Elaine was beginning to recover.

The following evening Miss Clarke came in and reported that she had had no luck with Mrs Reynolds whom she had rung and who had resolutely refused to meet her.

'Did she sound unbalanced?' asked Faye.

'It's hard to say on the telephone. But I'd say obstinate.'

'Leave it to me,' said Faye. 'I'll see what I can do.'

She noticed that Liz Clarke was wearing a new outfit and congratulated her on it.

'Are you going out?' she asked. 'You're looking very smart.'

The Welfare Officer blushed and looked ten years younger.

'Yes,' she said. 'Peter and I are going to the theatre and to dinner afterwards.'

Faye was delighted. They were two lonely people who had

for long enjoyed a lively love-hate relationship. It would be an excellent thing for both of them she thought; and then reproached herself for match-making.

That evening she discussed Elaine's case with Bill, not for the first time; for like many other people, he was deeply interested in the problem of euthanasia. He proffered her some valuable advice and she thought how helpful his objective views on her problems often were.

The next day, acting on his suggestion, she went down to Surrey where Mrs Reynolds lived in a pretty village near Farnham. Bill had suggested that he too should desert his office for the afternoon; they drove down together, making a detour to have a late and very agreeable lunch at Hampton Court on the way down. Faye had rung Mrs Reynolds that morning. She had used her most authoritative manner and finally Elaine's mother agreed to see her at four o'clock. She had asked the reason for Faye's visit and Faye had answered, 'It's about your daughter, Mrs Reynolds. I won't keep you long.'

'That's as well,' said Mrs Reynolds, 'As I have an appointment at half past four.' She had rung off without saying goodbye.

Bill drew up opposite the Reynolds' house. It was a prosperous looking example of stockbroker's Tudor. Faye walked up the brick path which led to the front door. After a few moments' delay, it was opened by Mrs Reynolds.

It was hard to believe that she was the mother of Elaine, who was thin and delicate looking, and must have taken after her father. Mrs Reynolds was a formidable good looking woman in her fifties, with a blue rinse and flyaway glasses. She was extremely well turned out. She seemed very controlled, but Faye could see, under the careful make-up, distinct signs of strain.

'Mrs Boswell?'

'Yes. I'm sorry to take up your time.'

'I don't imagine you'll be long,' said Mrs Reynolds coldly and took the Governor into a conventionally furnished sitting room, with lattice windows looking onto a garden. On a table stood a framed photograph of a middle-aged man.

'I was right,' thought Faye. 'Elaine is her father's daughter.'

'Will you sit down?' asked Mrs Reynolds. 'Now what is this all about?'

'About Elaine, naturally.'

'You said on the telephone that she has been suffering. In my opinion it's only right that she should.'

'You can't mean that!'

'I do indeed. I've said all along, I would almost have preferred it if those psychiatrists had found something wrong with her; instead of knowing she did what she did in cold blood.'

'Not in cold blood. I think it was out of love.'

'Self love perhaps. She had no feeling for anyone else.'

Faye managed with difficulty to control her temper.

'Mrs Reynolds,' she said. But Mrs Reynolds' cool facade was already beginning to crack.

'You have no right to come here,' she said to Faye, her voice rising.

'My only right is that I am deeply sorry for what has happened,' answered Faye. 'Both for you and for Elaine. I know that Elaine longs for you to write to her and to visit her.'

'I will not write or visit,' replied Mrs Reynolds. 'I've gone as far as I intend in helping Elaine. I have given the money, and I'll give no more.'

This extraordinary statement stopped Faye dead in her tracks. What did the woman mean?

'Money?' she asked puzzled.

'To the woman you sent. She told me of the hardship, the lack of food, proper clothing. I didn't refuse, but I told her it implied no forgiveness.'

'I don't understand. What woman do you mean?'

Mrs Reynolds looked angry. 'Why you sent her yourself. The assistant to the Chaplain at Stone Park. I gave her a hundred pounds for Elaine.'

'Reba,' thought Faye. 'I should have guessed she was up to something like this.' Aloud she said:

'I'm afraid you've been robbed, Mrs Reynolds. That woman must have been Reba Jowett. She's just finished two years for theft and false pretences.'

'You mean she had no connection with Elaine?'

'No, I don't mean that. Actually she was the only one among the prisoners who at first befriended your daughter.'

Mrs Reynolds stared at Faye, who continued:

'Elaine is not equipped for prison. Cut off from you, shunned by her own mother, it's with people like that, petty thieves and swindlers, that she's going to become involved. Is that what you want for her?'

Mrs Reynolds was becoming distressed now. Her voice was less firm as she said, 'She – she deserves it. They found her guilty.'

'Only, I think, because of what you said in court. Why did you do it? You knew it wasn't true to say what you did. If it hadn't been for that, the Judge would very likely have given her a suspended sentence.'

Mrs Reynolds was beginning to crumble before Faye's eyes.

'I – I never thought my husband was dying; why should I? He never told me. We were always planning things for next year, and I was sure he'd get better.'

'But Elaine knew?' asked Faye.

'Oh yes. Elaine knew.' Her voice was bitter. 'It was always "Elaine" from the moment he got ill. They shut me out. They have for years really. We had a son too, he was the one I understood, but he was killed in an accident when he was twelve. You don't know what it's like to lose a child.'

'I think I do,' said Faye gently. 'I lost my daughter when she was ten. It must mave been dreadful for you.'

'That was when I started all my good works, as my husband called them. He was so busy and Elaine was at school. Somehow I had to fill my life. After that, we seemed to become a divided family, and when he became ill, it was Elaine he turned to, not me.'

'Did he ever tell you that he wanted to die?'

There was a pause. Then Mrs Reynolds started to sob.

'Yes,' she said, 'He did. Our doctor had insisted on Elaine going out for two hours every afternoon, and the retired nurse who used to come and sit with him didn't turn up one day. He called for me and I went up. He seemed in great pain and he did . . .' she paused, 'he did say he couldn't stand it much longer.' She stopped and fumbled with her handkerchief.

'And what did you say?' Faye's voice was very gentle.

'I – I told him not to be silly. I didn't realize till afterwards that he meant it.'

For a moment Faye was silent. Then she said, driving home her advantage: 'Mrs Reynolds, would you be prepared to sign an affidavit to this effect? For, if you do, I think there is a strong hope of Elaine's case being reviewed.'

Mrs Reynolds blew her nose. 'I wouldn't mind having her back,' she said with a sniff. 'I've lost my daily and Elaine's good in the house.'

So she really only wants her back as an unpaid servant, thought Faye. Still, that is better than Stone Park. Keeping her temper she persuaded her hostess to let her make some tea for them both.

She then suggested that Mrs Reynolds should go and stay away for a while rather than remain in the house alone, and to this she agreed. Faye waited until she had rung her sister and arranged things. Her sister it appeared had been worrying over her and would be glad to fetch her tomorrow.

As Faye left, Mrs Reynolds said in a deliberately casual

voice, 'My sister lives in Suffolk. We'll be passing through London. How would it be if I visited Elaine tomorrow?'

Faye did not show how pleased she was. She merely said, 'A very good idea. Just ring and let me know what time and I'll arrange it with Miss Harker.'

And she walked across the village green to where Bill was waiting for her in the hotel.

As they drove home Faye told Bill what had happened. Mrs Reynolds would sign the affidavit tomorrow before she left.

'So she lied at the trial,' said Bill.

'I think it wasn't intentional. She was sick with jealousy, had been for years. Poor woman, she's not an attractive character, but I'm sorry for her.'

'I'm sorry for the girl,' said Bill. 'From what you tell me of Mrs Reynolds I think I'd rather stay inside.'

But Faye, who knew Stone Park better than Bill did, answered, 'You wouldn't, you know. Not at any price.'

When Janet Harker started work the next day, she had a telephone call from the Governor.

'I have to go to a meeting of the Prison Commissioners this morning,' she said. 'The Deputy will be taking Duties for me. I thought I'd let you know that Mrs Reynolds will probably be visiting her daughter this afternoon. As she hasn't even had her Standard Reception visit yet, I think we can allow this, can't we?'

Janet agreed enthusiastically, but added. 'The Chief may not be too keen. It's not a visiting day.'

'Then blame it on me,' answered Faye cheerfully. 'And tell Elaine, will you?'

'Of course,' said Janet, and thought, as she rang off, 'so she is bending the rules a bit for Elaine. I hope the Chief doesn't find out.'

That evening Faye sent Miss Clarke to see Elaine. She reported that the girl seemed almost cheerful.

One evening about a week later, Faye was going the rounds

and happened to visit the sewing shop where Elaine was now working. The Governor was glad to see that Elaine was talking to some of the other women. At the moment she seemed to be amused at something Barbara was saying, as she held up a shocking pink child's frock.

'I'nt that grand? I made it myself, for my little daughter.'

'Two mis-statements,' muttered the Chief's voice in Faye's ear. 'Firstly because Elaine did practically all the making, and secondly because Barbara hasn't got a daughter.'

Faye smiled briefly and passed on. Mrs Armitage was indeed a Job's comforter these days.

Mrs Reynolds had signed her affidavit the day after Faye had met her, and Elaine's solicitor at once set the Appeal in motion. In the course of three months it was heard, and, as the Governor had hoped, her sentence was suspended and she was freed.

Paradoxically, on the very day Elaine left, Reba returned. Mrs Reynolds had told the police about her and they had charged her with fraud. It took them some weeks to trace her, but after a long search they found her working in an old-worlde-gifte-shoppe in Rye. From there it was only a matter of days before she was back in Stone Park. She immediately asked to see the Chaplain, and very soon got back her Redband status, for, as he told the Governor, Reba was, despite her human frailties, the best chapel helper he had ever had.

To the surprise of the whole prison, and the relief of most of the inmates, the Chief suddenly disappeared from sight. For a day or two rumour ran rife through Stone Park. The Chief had been sacked . . . she was ill, even dying . . . she had won the Pools . . . she had done her old man in and was languishing in another goal. . . . Each rumour was more fantastic than the last.

On the third day the truth, which was sufficiently dramatic, was made known to the inmates. The Armitage daughter, Ellen, and her little girl had been in a car crash up North, where Ellen's 'husband' worked. He had been killed and she was badly injured, but the child was unhurt. Mrs Armitage had gone north at once.

Later, she wrote to Faye explaining things. She was staying in lodgings with her grandchild for a few weeks in order to visit Ellen in hospital each day. She apologised for having left so suddenly, but she knew that the Governor would understand that, very occasionally, one's family must come first. Surprisingly, she said in her letter:–

> 'I think Ellen and I understand each
> other now: we will never agree about
> some things, but I see where I went
> wrong in the past. I can hardly
> believe that I have my daughter back.'

She added that she would travel down, bringing Samantha, whilst Ellen was in a convalescent home. Later Ellen and the child would be staying with her for a while.

Mrs Armitage finished her letter:– 'When I get back, I hope you can find time to come to tea, I would like you to see Samantha, who is a little dear.'

Faye duly went to tea, and was amused, and rather touched, to see the formidable Chief in the role of Doting Grandmother.

When Mrs Armitage finally returned to the prison, after three weeks absence, there was a subtle change in her. Although she was as stern a disciplinarian as before, she now showed compassion to any woman in real distress. She was no longer so bad tempered with the staff, in fact she became positively human in her off-duty moments, and Martha Parrish grew quite irritated by her endless stories about her grand-daughter.

CHAPTER EIGHTEEN

Faye sat in the Mediterranean sun on the terrace of her hotel and sipped her campari. Mario had just brought her out some letters which had arrived by the morning's erratic post.

A boat with a red sail was tacking across the bay. The crew of two men waved and she waved back. Bill, and Paul, who had arrived back just in time to join his parents on their holiday. They were going to be late for lunch, thought Faye.

A pine cone dropped at her feet with a gentle plop; from the beach below came the distant chatter of cheerful Italian voices. The little town with its pink and yellow-ochre houses huddled closely together round the harbour, basked in the golden September sun.

Faye stretched herself lazily. She picked up the bundle of letters. They were all from the prison, for the Boswell's home post was not being forwarded.

'I'll leave them for now,' she thought, 'and walk down the hill to meet the others. But on the other hand . . . perhaps?'

She opened the one from the Radleys first. Everything was well under control, which was hardly surprising. The sting was in the tail of the letter: Beth was again pregnant. Faye would not be surprised if Charles soon moved to better things. It was high time that he had his own prison to run. How she would miss him. . . .

Mrs Armitage wrote a brief and rather dull letter. All was well, the new officers were satisfactory: and, just fancy! Ellen was thinking of taking up Welfare Work.

'I must remember to take that child a present,' thought Faye, and turned to the next letter, a depressed one from Janet Harker. Poor Janet, she was missing her Richard. There was a frivolous vulgar postcard from Peter Mayes and Liz Clarke sent when they had gone to Brighton for the day.

Faye did not see the little Italian fishing port any more, nor did she hear the local sounds. She was back in Stone Park. . . . She heard the clatter of the gates being locked and unlocked, the raucous laughter and the quarrels of the inmates. She thought of the problems, the punishments, and the few but worth-while triumphs.

She wondered whether the quiet civil servant who was in for a security offence, had been let out of solitary yet, or whether the other women were still bullying her: and whether the young Irish baby snatcher, who had arrived just before she left, had settled down yet.

She thought of the rapid increase in petty crime, especially among the very young. She thought with distress of the number of 'children' in prisons all over England. During the past year, at least five girls, aged from fourteen to sixteen had been given a harrowing taste of prison life, whilst awaiting trial, and only one of them had subsequently been convicted. It was a problem which worried Faye intensely, and one at which she was at loggerheads with the Government. Surely they would one day realise the priority of making different arrangements for these children?

A voice spoke behind her.

'Day dreaming, darling? That's the third time I've spoken to you.'

She looked up. Bill, sun burnt, with tousled hair and wearing a scarlet shirt, smiled down at her. Behind him Paul, a younger edition of Bill, grinned.

'What were you thinking about, Mum?' he asked.

Faye blinked, and came back to her holiday.

'Sorry, my darlings,' she said, with a distinct feeling of guilt. 'I was thinking, believe it or not, about Stone Park.'